Utopia,
Iowa

Utopia,
Iowa

BRIAN YANSKY

CANDLEWICK PRESS

YA

First edition 2015

Library of Congress Catalog Card Number 2014939349
ISBN 978-0-7636-6533-3

14 15 16 17 18 19 BVG 10 9 8 7 6 5 4 3 2 1

Printed in Berryville, VA, U.S.A.

This book was typeset in Scala and Agenda.

Candlewick Press
99 Dover Street
Somerville, Massachusetts 02144

visit us at www.candlewick.com

For my lovely sister, Jane Sharpe

Utopia, Iowa
From Wikipedia, the free encyclopedia

Utopia, Iowa, is one of the oldest settlements in Iowa. Located in the northeast corner of the state, the town is bordered by the Mississippi to the east, flat plains to the west, and rocky bluffs to the north and south. The population of Utopia is 5,001[1].

The town's largest employer is Nirvana College, which has an annual enrollment of between 2,000 and 2,300 students. Nicknamed the "Hogwarts of the Midwest" by a *New York Times* article[2], the college has a curriculum that includes classes in mind reading, fortune-telling, techniques for speaking to the dead, and Teleportation for Beginners.

The president of Nirvana College, Ted Houston, called His Holiness by his followers and the Cowboy Guru by the press, claims that the town of Utopia is located in a sacred place. He says a great city existed there once, long before recorded history. When pressed, he claims[3] that spirits — gods, even — built the city. These gods had the ability to take many forms, one of which was human. In addition, these deities could fly, move objects with their minds, view distant places without traveling there, and were possessed of other fantastical talents. However, there is absolutely no archaeological evidence, or any evidence whatsoever, to support Mr. Houston's claims of an ancient city.

However, the town is noted to have a milder climate than the rest of the Midwest for reasons that aren't entirely clear to meteorologists[4]. Also, people in this small community, as a rule, live remarkably long and healthy lives[5]. These two facts are sometimes cited as proof of Mr. Houston's assertion that Utopia, Iowa, is a sacred place.

Recently the town has become home to several successful Internet businesses, including Divination Plus and Charms for Travelers of Both the Physical and Spiritual Realms.

1. United States Census Bureau. "Demographic Trends of the Midwest." census.gov. 7 Feb. 2013. Retrieved 26 Dec. 2014.
2. Richardson, F. (14 July 2012). "The Hogwarts of the Midwest." *New York Times*, p. 8.
3. Richardson, F. (14 July 2012). "The Hogwarts of the Midwest." *New York Times*, p. 9.
4. Climate of Iowa. noaa.gov. Retrieved 11 Oct. 2013.
5. United States Census Bureau. "Demographic Trends of the Midwest." census.gov. 7 Feb. 2013. Retrieved 26 Dec. 2014.

1

I arrived late the first day of school, so I couldn't find my friends in the crowd that was herded into the cavernous auditorium for a pep rally first period of our first day back. When I was already in my seat, I saw Ash and Blake up near the front. Too late. I would have texted them, but school rules forbid any use of cell phones. You couldn't even look at your phone. Some of the teachers seemed to have a gift—or curse, depending on your point of view— for seeing cell phones in students' hands. In my opinion that was a very lame gift (or curse), but I kept my phone in my pocket.

Principal Thompson is a storky-looking guy with thick gray sideburns and abnormally large teeth (See *Scrooge*, 1951; writers: Charles Dickens, Noel Langley; stars: Alastair Sim, Jack Warner, Kathleen Harrison); he gave notoriously bad pep talks. His problem was that he had a monotone voice and bad posture, and the two together had an anti-pep effect.

I slipped lower and lower into my creaky auditorium seat, my yawns stretching themselves like lazy cats. Principal Thompson droned on and on, outlining the school rules and regulations, which seem to get stricter and stricter each year. Then he mentioned how the cafeteria would no longer serve creamed corn because it dries and sticks to surfaces and was hard to clean. I wasn't the world's biggest fan of creamed corn or anything, but for some reason, the banning of creamed corn was too much. Granted, I could have bumped past a row of knees to the aisle and quietly marched out of the auditorium; instead I took the less traveled road (thank you, junior English and Robert Frost) and boldly stood. I raised one closed fist into the air and shouted, "Give me creamed corn or give me death!" (Thank you, freshman history and Patrick Henry.)

Total silence. There is no silence like a room full of silent people.

My face reddened and I felt sweat break out around the collar of my new back-to-school shirt. I looked for escape, but the exits were impossibly distant from my position of humiliation.

Then a low murmur began. Then a chorus. "Creamed corn or death. Creamed corn or death." I realized I'd been holding my breath and once again joined others in the effortless inhale/exhale of air. Soon I was smiling. The whole school seemed to be chanting. Finally there was some pep in this pep rally. However, Principal Thompson was not looking pleased.

He raised his hands palms out, a regal gesture meant to order silence, but instead inspired louder chanting. Then he folded his arms. Too late I realized his devious strategy. He was waiting for us to become bored with chanting. Naturally, being teenagers, we did. I tasted the bitterness of failed revolution. I learned a hard lesson that day: real revolution needs more than creamed corn.

"Mr. Bell," he said, which just happens to be my last name. My first name is Jack, after Jack Kerouac, who is one of my father's three heroes. In case you're wondering, the other two are Mahatma Gandhi and Bruce Lee. "My office after the announcements are over."

It was not an unfamiliar place to me.

After the rally, as we made our way out, I received some slaps on the back and some "Awesome, dudes" and some cold stares from the cheerleaders whose idea of pep was not in line with mine (that day). I walked down the hall to the principal's depressingly small office, where he was already waiting for me.

We had a "nice" talk in which he did all the talking. He spoke first of school rules and starting the year off right. Then he reminded me of the Eleven Commandments. He paused to give significance to his ridiculous addition of one to the standard ten. Somehow even his pause had a dull edge to it. Then he said that the eleventh commandment was the one that Moses had not gotten around to writing down: "Be a good student so that you may later become a good teacher."

"What does that mean?" he asked me.

Rhetorical question, it turned out, because he didn't wait for me to answer. Over the next thirty minutes, he meandered through an explanation that left me more confused than when he'd begun — and had me nodding off. I shook myself awake as he sentenced me to ten hours of detention. I thought that excessive and told him so. He disagreed. I suggested a compromise of five hours. He became short with me and said this wasn't a negotiation.

"This last half hour should at least be counted as time served," I said, though really it should have been counted as at least five hours served, since it felt like that much.

"Good-bye, Mr. Bell," he said, sighing dramatically.

So the first day of my senior year, I earned my first detention of the new school year all because Principal Thompson was a bad public speaker with poor posture. After I sat my way through math, English, history, and biology, I sat my way through an hour of detention in a room with no windows. I read *Fahrenheit 451*, which seemed appropriate given my own recent run-in with totalitarian ruling forces. Today they were banning creamed corn; tomorrow it would be books.

I pointed this out to Mrs. Archer, the librarian who presided over detention and was a familiar after-school companion. She shook her head sadly. "Let me just remind you why you're here. Creamed corn. Does that make you think maybe your priorities are a little skewed, Jack?"

"Maybe," I admitted.

But I wondered if skewed priorities were a bad thing—which was probably just further proof that I had them.

2

When I got home to our large two-story house (which my dad says has character, another way of saying it's old) across the street from the greatest river in America, the mighty Mississippi, I had a close encounter of the third kind with my sister. By which I mean the seven-year-old, scrawny-limbed, towheaded girl tackled me, her technique NFL perfect though she weighed a paltry fifty-eight pounds. I landed hard on my side, but I lifted her off me a second later. She may have had a big personality, but she was still only fifty-eight pounds.

About a week earlier, I had made the mistake of ordering some old Pink Panther movies (1963–present; writers: Maurice Richlin, Blake Edwards; star: Peter Sellers) on Netflix and watching them with my sister. In the later ones, Inspector Clouseau, a detective of questionable skills, has an assistant named Cato, who has been ordered to attack Clouseau at unexpected times to keep him alert. I had given no such order to my baby sister, but she pretended I had. Nearly every time I came home, she waited somewhere in the house, hoping to catch me unaware and vulnerable to attack.

"I told you not to do that, Big Amanda," I said.

"I got you," she said.

I sighed. "Yes, you got me. Yes, you move like a cat."

That made her smile. It was one of our dad's phrases.

"I got you," she said again. "Now you have to watch TV with me."

"Is that a new rule?"

"Yes."

"I didn't get the memo," I said. "I have to decline."

"Ple-e-e-e-e-e-ease. Please. Please."

I said I had homework. Amanda's former compulsive love of musicals, particularly *The Sound of Music* (1965; writers: Howard Lindsay, Russell Crouse; stars: Julie Andrews, Christopher Plummer, Eleanor Parker), had been replaced by a new love: old, old TV shows, mostly old sitcoms my mom and dad had watched as kids. *Bewitched* was her current favorite.

"Ple-e-e-e-e-e-ease. Please. Please. We'll watch *Bewitched*."

"Homework," I repeated.

"I'll tell you a secret," she said.

Girls, even little girls, seem to know how to look like

1

they know more than they do. Most likely her secret would be some uninteresting gossip about another second-grader. I should have just ignored her. I should have. But.

"OK, but I'll do my homework while we watch *Bewitched*," I said.

"Deal." She stuck out her hand and we shook on it, her hand so tiny mine covered it like a catcher's mitt covers a ball.

"Tell me," I said.

"I saw a dead girl in your room," she said. "I'll turn on the TV. You make the popcorn."

Amanda skipped off to the living room, and a second later I heard the *Bewitched* music, which was not at all bewitching.

I considered this new information. On the one hand, it had been a long time since any girl at all had been in my room, so maybe I should have been grateful. On the other hand, a dead girl in my room meant complications. I was already dealing with detention, the start of senior year, and all kinds of questions about my future. I didn't need a dead girl, too.

But I had one. When it came to the dead, Amanda never lied.

}

I microwaved the popcorn and looked out the window over the sink into the backyard. Needed mowing. This was a fact I would not be pointing out to Dad, because as soon as I did, he'd assign the job to me.

Mom came into the kitchen carrying a load of laundry.

"Can you get the door, hon?" she asked.

I opened the door to the basement, where the washer and dryer were. Mom stood in the doorway, the laundry basket propped against her knee. She stared at me.

"Detention again?" she said. My mom is long all over: long face, neck, arms, and legs — in a Shelley Duvall in *The Shining* kind of way (1980; writers: Stephen King, Stanley Kubrick; stars: Jack Nicholson, Shelley Duvall, Danny Lloyd). She has almond-shaped eyes. She knows things she shouldn't.

"It wasn't my fault," I said.

She didn't give me a chance to explain about the principal's monotone voice or his stance on creamed corn.

"It's all right," she said. "I'm resigned to the fact that you'll be a career criminal. Just no guns. Promise me that."

"Mom."

"Promise."

"Right. No guns."

"That's a good boy," she said, and the stairs creaked as she disappeared into the cellar.

I carried the bag of popcorn into the living room, where Amanda was glued to the TV.

"I'm starving," she said. "I had a very tough day at school."

"Me, too," I said.

"Did you get pushed down during recess by Sam Yancey and told that you should watch where you're going?" she asked.

I had to admit that I had not. "You want me to beat him up?" I asked.

She considered this. In the past she'd always given a decisive "No" because she adhered to the code of non-violence preached by the great leader Mahatma Gandhi. His "An eye for an eye makes the whole world blind" was one of our father's favorite quotes, and Amanda took our father's attitudes very seriously.

"I guess not," she answered finally.

I made a mental note to make my offers of violence more carefully in the future. I sensed her loyalty to the code of nonviolence was being challenged by the behavior of boys.

"Popcorn," she ordered.

"Not so fast," I said, fighting the urge to do what she said because deep down I wanted to please her—almost always. "You get the popcorn when I get information."

"I'm watching," she said, staring intently at the TV screen, where Samantha was wrinkling her nose in order to perform some act of magic. The fact that I knew this depressed me.

I considered my next move carefully. My sister was ruthless when it came to secrets. Once she had the popcorn, she would hold on to her secret as long as possible and use it to get other favors from me.

I held the popcorn above my head and invited her to get it for herself.

"You're mean."

"Didn't I just offer to beat up a boy for you?"

She shrugged and pretended to turn her attention back to *Bewitched*.

"Smells so good," I said, taking a deep breath.

She snuck a look. Then she squinted at me in a Clint Eastwood in *The Good, the Bad and the Ugly* sort of way (1966; writers: Luciano Vincenzoni, Sergio Leone; stars: Clint Eastwood, Lee Van Cleef, Eli Wallach). Then she broke. Big dramatic sigh that went all the way up her back into her shoulders. "The ghost was on your bed in your room."

"What was she doing?"

"Just sitting on your bed."

"Old? Young? I need details."

"A teenager," she said, as if I was purposely being dense. "She was pretty, really pretty. She had long blond hair. She was different, though."

"How?"

"I don't know. She just looked different from most dead girls." Amanda's hands reached out longingly. "Popcorn. Need popcorn. Becoming zombie."

She pretended to keel over onto the sofa—which seemed more like the lying dead than the walking dead, but I kept this observation to myself. I gave her the popcorn, and she sat up and stuffed her mouth with a handful of kernels.

"Were you asleep when you saw her?" I asked.

"Nope," she said, flecks of partially chewed popcorn exploding out of her mouth like sparks from fireworks. She grinned, and then looked back at the TV screen and put her finger to her lips and whispered, "Shush, shush."

About an hour later, I heard our father pound down the stairs from his nap. He owned a bar, which was closed in the afternoons, and he always took what he called a siesta from about four to six. His bar is named Field of Dreams, after the movie *Field of Dreams* (1989; writers:

W. P. Kinsella, Phil Alden Robinson; stars: Kevin Costner, Amy Madigan, James Earl Jones), which is about an Iowa farmer who builds a baseball field for dead baseball players. The guy keeps hearing this whisper, "If you build it, they will come," and they do come, the dead baseball players, I mean, and they play games out there, too. Our dad's Field of Dreams was a coffee bar in the morning and a drinking bar at night. He closed it in the afternoons because he wanted a siesta, which showed the kind of businessman he was. A bad one.

"Hello, kids!" he shouted, bounding into the room. Dad is a shouter and a bounder. He got between Amanda and the TV and she complained and he told her he was more interesting than Samantha Stephens, which was true but not saying much. Then we had a conversation about tall people and short people because my father said short people liked TV too much.

"You can't like TV too much," Amanda said.

Our dad said she was a perfect example of a short person who was overly fond of what he called the idiot box.

"That's an idiotic thing to say," I said. "Sir."

"I'm not short," Amanda said. "For my age."

"And yet you like TV," our father said.

I was still trying to study, but I was sucked into the argument by my father's next statement, which was that short people have the advantage of their disadvantage. He made the case that short people needed to make up for being short and so try harder.

"Look at Napoleon," he said. "He would never have conquered his own backyard if he'd been tall."

He and I argued while Amanda scooted over and watched more *Bewitched*. The problem was our dad enjoyed an argument and sometimes said things just to irritate me into reactions. Oddly, I didn't hate him for it. Stockholm syndrome, maybe?

I imagined that Dad was getting a lot of argument practice at his bar, which he'd only opened a year earlier, when he went through what our mom called a "midlife crisis" and quit being a carpenter and furniture maker, saying he needed to fulfill his dream of being a bar owner now or he never would. The problem was the bar wasn't profitable. He'd never made a fortune as a carpenter, but we'd gotten by. Now we weren't getting by. Mom was worried. I was worried.

Mom interrupted Dad's new topic—which was his observation that road trips didn't have the romance for my generation that they did for his—by calling us in to dinner.

"Amanda saw a ghost in my room today," I told our parents as I sat at the hourglass-shaped table my father had built, a beautiful work of art but, like all his furniture, a little difficult to use. Everyone had vegetarian food in front of them but me. Our mother accommodated my carnivorous preference by making me pot roasts and hamburgers and chicken to go with whatever arrangement of vegetables they were eating.

Amanda frowned. "I didn't say you could tell them."

"Were you asleep, sweetie, when you saw this ghost?" Mom asked.

Amanda's lower lip came out, as it did when she was upset. Mom would often warn her that her lip could get stuck there permanently if she wasn't careful. "And that would be a tragedy, sweetie," she'd add.

"I already told him," she said, poking me in the shoulder.

"Don't do that," I said to Amanda. Turning to Mom, I said, "She wasn't asleep."

"You know how I feel about dead people wandering around the house," Mom said.

"I didn't ask her in," I said.

"Are you sure? I don't see how she got in if she wasn't asked."

"Not by me," I said. Not that I would mind having a girl in my room; I just wanted her to be alive.

Mom looked at Amanda.

"No," she said. "I don't like dead people wandering around the house, either."

"I'll check the charms," Mom said. "They simply don't make charms the way they used to. God, listen to me. I sound like my mother."

"You'll figure it out," Dad said. "'Strength does not come from physical capacity. It comes from an indomitable will.'"

"Mahatma Gandhi," I said.

"Bruce Lee," Amanda said.

"I'm going to have to go with Amanda," our mother said. "Bruce Lee."

We'd played this game since I was a little older than Amanda.

"Congratulations, son," Dad said.

"It really sounded like Bruce Lee," Mom said, patting Amanda consolingly on the shoulder.

After dinner, Dad challenged us all to a game of Risk. I didn't really feel like it, but his boasts about his success at world domination the last time his armies had taken the field of battle convinced me he needed to be put in his place.

"I'm the king of the world!" he said.

"That guy who directed *Titanic*," Mom said (1997; writer: James Cameron; stars: Leonardo DiCaprio, Kate Winslet).

"James Cameron," I said.

"That's not a real quote," Amanda said.

"Correct," our father said. "It's a fake quote. I will be king of the world, though."

"You talk the talk," Mom said. "Let's see if you can walk the walk."

In fact, he could. The rest of us might be able see dead people, like the kid in *The Sixth Sense* (1999; writer: M. Night Shyamalan; stars: Bruce Willis, Haley Joel Osment, Toni Collette) — among other things — but when it came to conquering countries and wiping out armies, Dad could walk the walk.

The city is magnificent. Magic sparkles off the surfaces of all things. The streets are wide when they need to be wide and narrow when they need to be narrow, and the buildings seem to touch the sky. There are markets where those who dwell outside the city bring their wares; these visitors are always careful to be on their best behavior, for all know that even the weakest city dweller could stop their heart with a single look. Those outside the city call the city dwellers gods, but they are not gods, though they are not human, either.

The city dwellers call all those who live outside the city short-livers because the city dwellers live thousands of years. And when their end nears, the strongest of the strong can live on if they're willing to take other bodies, if they're willing to end lives to extend their own.

The queen is not so old, but the king is one of those who must take and wear new bodies in order to live on. Usually he takes one of the short-livers, but sometimes he will take the body of a city dweller because they last so much longer. He wears them like clothes, discarding them when they are worn out or the mood strikes him. His long life has made him very powerful. This and his need for bodies and his temper make him feared by all.

Even the queen fears him, which has made her careful except in one rather significant respect. She has fallen in love with a beautiful youth, a short-liver who is the son of one of the chiefs of a minor tribe. Already she has betrayed the king with him.

She wakes in fear and goes to sleep in fear. It is madness to see the boy. She tells herself it must end. But still she goes to him. Again and again.

4

My mother was angry with me the next morning because I wouldn't get up, but I told her to try sleeping in a bed where a ghost had been. All night long, I kept waking up shivering; it was freaking Alaska in my dreams. I ended up sleeping on the sofa in the living room.

"You should have just done that in the first place," Mom said as I sat at the kitchen table. She'd been dealing with ghosts since she was eight years old, so she wasn't sympathetic about incorporeal inconvenience.

"I'll go see your grandmother today," Mom added. "We'll get some stronger charms. There won't be any more ghosts in your bed."

Then she had to leave for her part-time job as assistant to the richest woman in town, Mrs. Piermont Morgan. For twenty hours a week, that mean old lady abused my mother. She didn't even pay her that well. When I asked why she put up with Mrs. Piermont Morgan, Mom said that Mrs. Morgan needed her. That was not a good reason as far as I was concerned. I'm sure Attila the Hun "needed" someone, too.

I was ten minutes late getting to Mr. Van Horn's class, and he gave me that evil look he gives everyone who walks in late, as if he is doing his best to make them a victim of instantaneous combustion.

"That's one, Mr. Bell," he said.

He called us all by our last names like Sir does in *To Sir, with Love* (1967; writers: E. R. Braithwaite, James Clavell; stars: Sidney Poitier, Judy Geeson, Christian Roberts).

"Sorry," I said. I was sorry he had the unjust policy of taking off points every time a student was late. Not so sorry to miss a few minutes of English.

I sat at a desk near the back, my usual seating preference in a classroom. Mr. Van Horn had decided we would start the semester by reading *The Great Gatsby*, which earned him nods of approval from both the nonreaders (thin novel) and most of the readers (already read it). I fell into the second category.

Mr. Van Horn rambled on about the themes of *Gatsby*: romantic love and class in America and the American Dream. Mr. Van Horn did love books. He wore black pointy shoes, and when he got excited, his heels lifted off the floor. He got excited about books a lot. It was one of the things I really liked about him. And to be honest, I liked English, too—just not his attendance rules.

I listened, but I also looked out the window and wondered about that ghost on my bed. No, not wondered. Worried. It had to hurt her to be in our house. There were charms and other things to keep ghosts out. She must have had a very good reason to force her way in. And that worried me.

"Mr. Bell," Mr. Van Horn said. "What is so interesting out that window?"

I couldn't say that I'd been thinking about a dead girl. I had enough trouble getting dates. So I looked harder to try to see something interesting out there.

"End of summer," I said.

Everyone looked out the windows. Fall was blowing in. The leaves were shivering. It wouldn't be long before they started changing colors.

"Yes, yes," Mr. Van Horn said dismissively, because he knew better than anyone about the changing weather. He had, according to Gram, the gift—or curse, depending on your point of view—of smelling what the weather would be, particularly when it was changing or dangerous. Our town was too small to have local TV news, but we did have a radio station, and Mr. Van Horn would tell them when dangerous weather was coming. He was always right. Always.

"Back to *Gatsby*. What do you think, Mr. Bell? Is true love real?"

There were some snickers. True love? Seriously? But before I considered the potential fallout from an honest answer, I answered honestly. Stupid.

"Yes."

The snickers became nervous laughs. There were a few "Awws" from the sarcastic, mostly boys, and a few moonish stares from the romantic, mostly girls. Dickerson, the kind of jock who helped create and maintain the jock stereotype, said, "True love lasts as long as a good—"

"That's about twenty seconds for you," Kayla said.

The laughter pretty much ended class, because the bell went off before Mr. Van Horn could regain control. As we shuffled out, he shouted that we were to read two *Gatsby* chapters by next class.

"Hey, lover boy," Dickerson said, passing by with his redheaded sidekick, Bill Wayne, who added, "Lover boy," in his usual echo of Dickerson.

It was an unoriginal nickname, but that wouldn't matter if they were able to get others to start using it. That would be irritating. What had I been thinking? I knew, though, didn't I? A fact I would deny under the most severe torture imaginable. Rip out my heart. No comment. Tear out my soul. No comment. Chop off my head. Really—no comment.

I knew any attempt at denial or counterattack would

only motivate Dickerson, so I tried a mysterious look, like I'd had erotic experiences they couldn't even imagine. They laughed at me.

Still, as I walked down the hall, I felt a strange exhilaration thinking of my admission. It had felt good saying it out loud. Good and bad. How did I know true love was real? Easy. I'd felt it.

5

Ash, my best friend, stood at the smokers' wall, which was around the corner from the auditorium and out of view of the administration offices. Butts littered the ground all around her. I shook a cigarette out of the crumpled pack I carried around and held it just like you would if you were going to smoke—except that I didn't. I had tried to become addicted to cigarettes when Ash became addicted. I thought it would be an act of solidarity. But, despite my efforts, I was immune to cigarettes' well-documented addictive properties.

Ash was tall and thin, with hair that changed color every month. That day it was purple. Her grandparents on both sides were Russian, and there was something exotic in the shape of her face. She had a pretty mouth and big gray eyes. Some guy, trying to pick her up, had once said she could be a Bond girl, and she had quoted Angelina Jolie at him: "I don't want to be a Bond girl. I want to be Bond."

"It's like fraud," she said, gesturing at the cigarette between my fingers. "You're making a mockery of rebellion and addiction."

The wind picked up and the trees shivered.

"Maybe they deserve to be mocked," I said.

She made an unattractive sound, a snort really, and flicked her ash. Ash was an expert ash flicker.

I inspected my unlit cigarette. "There was a ghost in my bed last night."

"Male or female?"

"Girl ghost. Amanda saw her. Hot one, from the sound of it."

"I know it's been a while since you've had a girlfriend, but—"

I wanted to say something about her boyfriend selection, but instead I said, "Not that long."

Condescending smile. She was very good at them. "Just one more reason you've got to get out of here, Jack. Dead girls showing up in your bed."

Ash had already applied for early admission to Stanford, and given her GPA and test scores, she would probably get in. I hadn't applied anywhere or even thought seriously about applying. I wasn't even sure I wanted to go to college. Everyone else was sure for me: teachers, counselors, parents, aunts, uncles, friends, Gram. Even

Amanda talked about my going off to college as if it were a given.

Ash said, "Nathaniel thinks you have to move to LA if you really want to work in film. You can live there for a year and get in-state tuition and then go to UCLA or USC. I could come down and see you sometimes."

Nathaniel was Ash's obnoxiously cool college boyfriend (University of Iowa). He was a philosophy major who I had diagnosed, after taking a psychology course last semester, as having a classic narcissistic personality. Ash was ten thousand times too good for him.

"*If* I want to work in film?" I said, stung by the betrayal of her doubt and irritated that she'd been talking to Nathaniel the narcissist about me.

"You know what I mean. You've got to get out of Utopia to write your screenplays."

"A dead girl could be in my bedroom anywhere, you know," I said.

"Maybe. Maybe not."

Sometimes a person's gift—or curse, depending on your point of view—left them when that person left Utopia. Sometimes it didn't. I worried I would see a lot more dead people in a place with a lot more live ones. I worried about being in a place where I didn't know anyone else who saw dead people, didn't have any gifted—or cursed, depending on your point of view—family or any friends. I knew Utopia, and Utopia knew me. Did I really want to give that up?

The bell rang. We walked up to the front door, Ash still talking about my murky future. I kept a neutral silence. The halls were full of bodies going in every direction, bunching up into gridlock at the main stairway. Locker doors slammed and voices echoed like dropped coins. As we made our way down the hall through groups of students toward White's Twentieth-Century American History class, Ash said, "I just don't want you to stay here and end up working for your dad."

"Would it really be so bad?" I said. Rhetorical question. The answer was no. I could do a lot worse. I might.

"You know I love you like a brother," she said (I winced but tried to play it off like I was about to sneeze), "but if you let yourself get stuck in this town, I'll have you kidnapped. No joke. I know people."

She did. Ash's mom is originally from a Chicago family Ash called "midlevel Russian Mafia." She'd run away to Iowa when she was a teenager. She was a lawyer now. She did a lot of work for Nirvana College.

"One great thing about writing screenplays is that I can do it anywhere," I pointed out, and not for the first time.

She frowned. "You can't stay here. You have to go out into the world to know what you want from it." She raised her bare arms into the air and closed her eyes. "'The answer is out there, and it's looking for you, and it will find you if you want it to.'"

"I can't believe it."

"Believe it."

"You're quoting Trinity to Neo? You don't even like that movie." (*The Matrix,* 1999; writers: Andy and Lana Wachowiski; stars: Keanu Reeves, Carrie-Anne Moss, Laurence Fishburne.)

Ash had said *The Matrix* was overrated, even though she'd never actually seen it. "That's *why* I won't see it," she'd said when I pointed this fact out to her. That was Ash. Maddening with her illogical logic.

Now she shrugged. "Nathaniel had to watch it for one of his philosophy classes, so I watched it with him."

"Awesome professor."

Ash raised an eyebrow. "Nathaniel says *The Matrix* is like Philosophy for Dummies."

That sounded like Nathaniel.

"So why are you quoting it?" I asked.

"I kind of like it," she admitted.

"I kind of like it, too," I said.

We smiled but then realized how comfortable we were smiling at each other and became uncomfortable.

When we got to class, Mr. White was talking to Michael Bump about Michael's father, who was going to be shot out of a cannon that weekend. Mr. Bump was an adventurer who refused to leave Utopia for his adventures. That was how he put it. So he did things like swim from bank to bank of the Mississippi a hundred times, perform acrobatics in an airplane above Utopia, and do skydiving stunts.

"I don't understand how he can be sure to land safely," Mr. White said.

"If he's right on, he lands on the net. If he goes too far, he lands in the Mississippi."

Mr. White, being a teacher, did what teachers do and asked the obvious question. "What if he doesn't go far enough?"

"Except for that," Michael said. "He doesn't have that worked out."

SCREENPLAY IDEA: A movie about a man named Bump who grows up in a small town wanting to be a daredevil. But he won't leave the little town he's grown up in. So he does these amazing tricks just for the people in that town, even though all these big offers come to him from Las Vegas and Hollywood and New York. Why won't he take the big money? It turns out he's afraid of crowds. He can jump out of planes without a parachute (he catches up to it on the way down), be buried alive in a coffin, be handcuffed and put in a trunk dumped into the Mississippi, but he's afraid of crowds. Can his high-school sweetheart help him to overcome his fears and follow his dreams, or is he doomed to perform for smaller and smaller crowds who have seen it all before?

The second bell went off and we took our seats.

Mr. White was about to start talking about history-type things when he was interrupted by the intercom and

Vice Principal Sanderson's voice with the daily announcements.

Vice Principal Sanderson had been a disc jockey at radio stations in Iowa City and Chicago when he was young. When his voice came over the intercom, he sounded like he thought he was on the radio. "Hello, Utopia High listeners!" he shouted. "Vacation is over and we're back. Time to talk the talk of school days. Be all you can be. Ignore, please, the moaning coming from the cafeteria. It has, we're told, something to do with the heater. It is not anything to worry about and it is certainly not, as one rumor has it, a banshee. We want no further rumors started, please. It will be fixed shortly. And something for you faculty out there. Meeting at four o'clock in the auditorium." He went on like this for about two or three minutes and then he ended with his usual "Rock on, Utopia High!"

Mr. White shook his head.

"What's a banshee?" one of the twins, Nathan, asked. Nathan and Jason are what I called Rasta Jocks, weed-loving football players.

"A ridiculous Irish myth," Mr. White said.

Sure, I thought. *Ridiculous if you've never seen one. Terrifying if you have.*

He went on. "A fairy woman who screams. She's supposed to predict death."

Everyone became very still, as if we were gathered

around a campfire and about to be told a scary story. This seemed to inspire Mr. White.

"She wails and wrings her hands and tells of death. But in the old tales of Ireland, she was more likely to be washing human heads and limbs and bloodstained clothes in streams turned red. She'd appear just before a battle. Sometimes young. Sometimes old. Often fearsome to look at."

He paused and all of us were holding our breath.

"But it's just a story, of course. Let's talk about some real history now. No more banshees."

We heard a wailing then, so loud it felt like the floor was shaking. I gripped my desk and felt something crawl up my back. I jumped out of my seat. Several others jumped out of their seats, too. No one laughed. After a few more seconds, the wailing stopped and we sat back down.

"Those old pipes," Mr. White said, shaking his head.

I knew that Mr. White believed he was hearing old pipes and that there were plenty of people in the room who heard what he heard and not what I heard because they'd learned how not to see and hear the strange things that happened in our town. But others were upset and shaken.

"Does the banshee always mean death?" Whisper Wainwright asked. She was a small, thin girl with a reedy voice. Very quiet, hence the nickname. Her real name was Sandra.

"It's a story," Mr. White said. "Just a story."

Jason made a ghostly moan that sounded nothing like the banshee. A few people laughed. Not many.

"All right," Mr. White said. "That's enough."

Then he started telling us that this semester would cover the period from 1900 up to the 9/11 terrorists' attacks. He said it was a lot to cover, but it would make for an exciting experience. "We'll start with a description of what the world looked like back in 1900. Horses and buggies were still used, even in big cities. No electricity. They had gas lamps. There were forty-five states, seventy-six million people in America. A man could expect to live about forty-six years and a woman about forty-eight, if they had the money for medical care. Most didn't."

Jason raised his hand and, when called on, asked Mr. White if Kent State was really as bad as people said. This was a strategic move. Mr. White was an expert on the sixties and had written several books on that decade. He loved to talk about it. If Jason could succeed in getting Mr. White sidetracked, there'd be that much less info that could be covered on the first test.

"Later," he said, brushing away the question with a swat of his hand. Jason slumped back in his chair.

"Now, it's true that even in the early 1900s, people in Utopia lived long past their fifties. The average age of a citizen was around a hundred even then. This is likely thanks to the town's small gene pool, which is predisposed to longevity."

That was one theory. The other theory was that longevity was yet another Utopian gift—only this one seemed to be given to everyone born in Utopia. But people like Mr. White ignored this possibility.

He went on to mention the magicians who were born in Utopia before 1900 and became well known in the first decades of the twentieth century. Some nearly as famous as Houdini, he said.

"Of course, the fact that there are several families with a tradition of performing magic tricks—and I want to stress the word *tricks* here—has contributed to the superstitions surrounding our town."

Mr. White often did this. He made arguments against Utopians having special gifts, and he tried to convince us that strange things didn't happen in our town. For a man who loved facts, he managed to ignore some pretty big ones about Utopia.

Denial, as Gram likes to say, isn't just a river in Egypt.

The bell rang and we crowded out of the room, unusually quiet. I walked down to the cafeteria, like a lot of people seemed to be doing, but I didn't hear anything. They must have fixed the "pipes." According to Gram, the school maintenance guy, Henry, had a gift— or curse, depending on your point of view—for setting broken things right and ridding buildings and houses of unwanted visitors from the world beyond this one. The two kind of went together—in Utopia.

• • •

After school I skipped detention to play cards with Will, Blake, and Chris (not Ash, who said cards were a waste of time). We played at Chris's house, in the basement.

When talk turned to the pipes/banshee, Will told us that one of his grandmothers was Irish and claimed that her own mother had once seen a banshee when she was a girl just before her father drowned in Lake Michigan on a fishing trip.

"You really think it was a banshee we heard?" Chris asked.

"Did that sound like pipes to you?" Will said.

"There's no such things as banshees," Blake said. He was in the denial camp.

"Sure didn't sound like pipes," I said.

"This town," Blake said. "I will be so glad to get out of this town."

"You'll miss the sweet sound of banshees, though," I said.

"I won't miss one thing."

"Can we just play cards?" Chris said.

I won about ten dollars at poker. Chris won the most, which was almost always the case and made me wonder if he had a gift—or curse, depending on your point of view—for knowing more about other people's cards than he should.

Chris's mom came downstairs after we'd been playing for a while and told Chris he needed to rush down to

Green's Grocery because Mr. Wilson was going to get some strawberry preserves in very shortly. This broke the game up because once we heard Mr. Wilson was going to have preserves, we all knew we'd have to rush down there, too. His preserves were famous in Utopia. When you ate them, you felt like everything was right with the world. Some people claimed that they even helped you think more clearly. Mr. Wilson only made a few batches a year, and they never lasted long, even with Green's Grocery's limit of two jars per customer.

"How'd your mom know they were going to be at Green's?" I asked Chris as we left.

"Lucky guess," he said.

"Runs in the family," I said. "You're pretty good at guessing when to hold and when to fold."

"That's called skill, my friend."

"Is that what you call it?"

"Whenever anybody asks," he said.

He was reminding me that I was being rude. People with gifts — or curses, depending on your point of view — were supposed to know better than to ask about another person's special talents. I did know better. I just didn't like losing at cards.

The four of us headed for Green's Grocery, beating the rush because of Chris's mother. I bought two jars and rode home. I texted Mom on the way to tell her about Mr. Wilson's preserves. I decided not to tell her about the possible banshee. She had enough to worry about these days; I didn't want to add a screaming woman portending death to the list.

But I did worry. I'd heard a banshee once before, and she'd been right that time: one of my favorite uncles was dead a day later. Who was this banshee screaming about?

6

I made it as far as our living room before Amanda jumped
me from the big armchair next to the kitchen doorway.

She got me in a choke hold. I struggled to breathe.
Inspector Clouseau would have shaken Cato off, but as
much as I wanted to, I couldn't do that to my little sister.
I tried to pull her arms away, but she was surprisingly
strong. Unnaturally strong. I imagined the headline:
"Teen Strangled by His Seven-Year-Old Sister."

I was frantic to breathe; I fell back onto the sofa.
Another headline went through my mind: "Bully Teenage
Brother Sentenced to Life in Prison for Squashing Little
Sister to Death During Horseplay."

She lost her hold.

"That hurt," she said from under me.

I rolled off the sofa and onto my hands and knees and gasped for air. When I could breathe, I said, "Good one. You nearly got me there, Cato."

"I'm telling Mom you squashed me."

"Would Cato run off and tell his mom he got a little squashed?"

She considered this. She seemed torn.

"You have to watch TV tonight with me, then," she said.

"Dad's right. You watch too much TV."

"Mom!" she shouted.

"OK," I said, raising my hands in mock surrender, though come to think of it, it wasn't really mock.

I heard the creaky front door open and close. Dad shouted that he was home — I'd thought he was upstairs deep in siesta, but I guess he'd gone out — and Amanda, like a puppy, ran to greet him.

I went into the kitchen and gave Mom the two jars of Mr. Wilson's jam. She kissed me on both cheeks like we were French. Both my mom and dad like to do that. It was weird, but when you were around weird all the time, it became almost normal. Which was kind of a troubling thought.

"Your family thanks you," she said.

"Amanda is stronger than she should be, you know."

"I know," she said. "That girl is a prodigy in many ways. Did you notice the doors?"

"I didn't have time before I was attacked."

"Do you want me to have a talk with your little sister about attacking her big, strong brother? Maybe I can get her to go easy on you."

"That's very funny, Mom," I said, and went and looked at the doors. There were these little troll dolls hooked to the walls above the doorways. They were naked and had purple hair.

"Those are the most frightening charms you could find?" I said as I came back into the kitchen. It smelled good in that room. The kitchen was always my favorite room. I grabbed a few Oreos from the cookie jar.

"We're not trying to frighten. We're trying to keep out things that shouldn't come in. These will. By the way, Gram wants you to go see her."

"OK."

"Tonight."

"Why?" I said.

"She was being secretive."

"I've got homework."

"I'd go if I were you," she said. "You don't want one of her unannounced dream visits, do you?"

Gram did that sometimes. The first time was when I'd avoided seeing her because I knew she was mad at me for stealing strawberries from Mr. Wilson's garden. I'd stolen them as an experiment to see if the strawberries, by themselves, could make me feel good. They didn't—though they did taste pretty wonderful. But there was a price. Gram showed up in one of my dreams. At first she was some cross between a snake and an eagle, and she swooped down right next to me. I may have screamed. Then she turned into Gram and told me to stop screaming like a little girl. Then she said, "You think this is bad? It's not wise to steal from Mr. Wilson, Jack. If you weren't my grandson, he'd be here himself, and it would be much, much more unpleasant than this."

She turned back into the terrifying bird-snake thing and flew out of my dream. She'd visited me three more times, for various reasons, since then. It was never fun.

"Fine," I said to Mom.

"Good," she said.

Mom asked me about school, and I told her about Ash threatening to have me kidnapped if I didn't leave Utopia when we graduated.

"She cares about you," she said.

Sure, I thought. *Threatening to have the Russian Mafia kidnap a person is a sure sign of affection.*

"You agree with her?"

"You know I'm against violence."

"Mom," I said. OK, it was sort of a whine but a manly whine.

"I want you to do what you want to do. And if what you want to do can't be done here in Utopia, then you have no choice but to leave. You should go to college, Jack. Writers need to know a few things."

"That's why we have the Internet."

"You need an education. You need college. You're a

smart kid and you're a lot more prepared than I was. You need to get out of here, Jack. You can always come back, you know." She chopped some yellow and green squash. She was very fast. She swung back toward me, carelessly pointing the knife. "We can go see Penny if you want."

Penny was a fortune-teller. She also had a nursery. She was very good with plants and visions of the future. It was a small town; a lot of people needed more than one talent to get by.

"Ash thinks maybe I should move to LA, get in-state tuition, and go to film school there."

"Not a bad plan," Mom said.

"Trying to get rid of me?" I said.

"Of course not."

"Maybe I like it here."

"Maybe," she said, but she didn't sound sure.

Thinking about the future, my future, made me nervous. I changed the subject: "How was your day with the Wicked Witch?"

"Oh, you know, fed the army of flying monkeys and turned a few princes into frogs and made some poisoned soup for her enemies."

"Average day, then," I said.

"Funny, she asked about you."

"What's funny about that?"

"She never asks about you or about anyone, really. I mean, not Dad or Amanda or even Gram. She asked if you'd been acting strangely."

41

"What did you say?"

"How could I tell?"

"Funny, Mom."

"You know what I really said?"

"Do I want to know?"

"You seem perfectly normal to me. And adorable."

I rolled my eyes.

Dad came into the kitchen carrying Amanda.

"Look what I found out in the living room. A gigantic bug."

"I'm not a bug," Amanda said.

"It's not a species I'm familiar with, though," he said, looking over Amanda's shoulder at Mom and me.

"I'm not a bug," she said again.

"It's one that clings. I know that much. It's a clinging bug."

"Be careful she doesn't get her arms around your neck," I warned.

"Right. Poisonous."

"I'm not poisonous," she said.

"Naturally you wouldn't tell us if you were."

"I'm not."

"All non-bugs in this house need to go wash their hands because dinner is almost ready," Mom said.

Amanda let go of our father and dropped. She shouted that she would race me to the bathroom. She was already running. I walked because I knew I couldn't catch her. I looked back and saw my parents kiss.

They don't give each other little pecks like most of my friends' parents do. They do some serious kissing. Sometimes when my dad comes home they practically make out in the kitchen. It's disturbing. It's embarrassing. But every once in a while, and this was once in a while, it made me sort of happy.

1

After dinner Amanda and I went off to watch *The New Voice* and my parents got into an argument over money—or the lack thereof. I guess they had occasionally argued over little stuff like the population of China or whether 10,000 Maniacs was a better band than Crash Test Dummies, but their only serious arguments were over money. And it had only gotten more serious since Dad bought the bar.

Amanda and I pretended not to hear them. I turned up the TV, which had this guy on doing a rap version of "Somewhere Over the Rainbow." "Yo, dawg, somewhere over that rainbow, skies be blue."

Mom said, "I'm tired of being the one who has to worry about whether we can pay our bills every month. Field of Dreams isn't working."

"It's close to working," Dad said. "We need to give it a chance."

"We've given it a chance. Anyway, you don't need to be serving coffee and liquor; you need to be making things."

"I've always wanted a bar."

"You make beautiful furniture," she said. "And you like doing remodeling jobs when you get into them. You made good money sometimes." She sighed—loudly enough that we could hear it over the TV. "We've almost run out of savings. You have to face facts. Field of Dreams was a mistake."

"It's my dream," he said.

"We're sinking."

"We could borrow from the college fund," he said. "Anyway, Jack wants to be a screenwriter. He doesn't need college for that. Jack Kerouac only—"

"Went to college for two years," she said. "Like you."

"There are other ways to learn. I learned a lot more hitching around the country than I ever learned in school."

"Jack's going to college. We aren't touching the college fund."

"The bar is my dream," Dad said.

He used to say Mom was his dream. Now the bar was.

"Your dream is becoming my nightmare. How do you think that makes me feel?"

"Jealous, from the way you're talking."

Furious whispers. Whisper-shouting.

The rapper: "That's right, dawg, them skies be blue. I know I flew. Somewhere over that rainbow. Blue as blue."

Amanda kept her eyes glued to the TV, pretending she couldn't hear a thing, pretending skies be blue.

"You think he'll win?" I said.

"Actually," she said, "he's actually very bad."

"Yeah," I said, "he actually is."

My cell rang. Ash. I didn't answer it. But my third eye took over—without any conscious decision on my part—and I saw her, phone to ear, looking cute in a short dress and boots and lying on her bed.

"I'm just tired!" Mom shouted. "I'm just very tired of it all."

Silence. Silence like a loaded gun. Silence that seemed to get louder and louder.

"You know what we need?" Dad said.

"I think I do," Mom said.

"Ice cream."

Not the answer Mom was looking for.

"I don't feel like it."

"You say that now, but never underestimate the power of double chocolate chip and bing cherry."

Amanda and I weren't listening to the show anymore. We knew that if Mom agreed to ice cream, the argument was over.

I felt Amanda's little hand slide into mine. I was no mind reader, but I thought she might be praying.

"Fine," Mom said. "You buy."

We had ice cream at the Purple Cow, a block south of campus. Dad said to Amanda and me, "You know your mom and I adore each other, don't you? 'Honest differences are often a healthy sign of progress.'"

Sometimes I worried that my father's heroes' sayings, wise though they were, were not enough.

"Mahatma Gandhi," I said.

"I know who it isn't," Mom said. "It isn't Jack Kerouac."

"Actually," Amanda said, "it could be Bruce Lee."

"Gandhi," Dad said. "He knew how to negotiate."

I got a text from Ash asking me if I wanted to come over. This time I forced my third eye not to look beyond what the other two could see. I texted back that I had to go to my grandmother's.

When I looked up, I saw a girl's face against the glass to my right. Dead girl, I thought, but something felt undead about her. For a second it felt like her hand came through the glass and reached into me and grabbed my heart. I couldn't breathe. It only lasted a second; the whole experience was so strange that it almost felt like I'd imagined it.

"What's wrong?" Mom said.

"Nothing."

"You saw something," she said.

"Just a dead person," I said.

"Where?"

I gave a lazy point.

"You're sure she was dead?"

"Yes. No. I'm not sure."

"Carter, cover Amanda's ears," Mom ordered.

"No-o-o-o-o-o-o-o," my sister moaned.

"Sorry," Dad said as he put his hands over Amanda's ears.

"Your grandmother said no ghost could have gotten through those charms. She thinks it was something else."

"Like what?"

"That's the question. She said something not alive but not dead. That's why she gave us the trolls. Those little trolls are supposed to be strong enough to keep out more than dead people. What did you just see, Jack?"

"I'm not sure," I admitted. "A girl. I don't know if she was dead. I thought so. Then I didn't."

I took a long drink of water. Amanda said she'd seen a ghost in my room. Amanda was very familiar with ghosts, so this . . . whatever . . . was powerful enough to fool her *and* break through Gram's charms. That was powerful.

"She's probably just some poor lost spirit," I said.

Mom looked worried, and we had enough family drama going on; I decided not to tell her about the spirit reaching into me and grabbing my heart.

"Done?" Dad said.

Mom nodded.

He took his hands off Amanda's ears.

"I hate it when you do that," Amanda said, glaring at all of us.

They let me off at Gram's. Her house was about three blocks from the Nirvana campus.

"I'll ride the bike home," I told them. I kept an old beater bike at Gram's that I'd ride home if I got left off there.

"I want to see Gram, too," Amanda said.

"Not tonight," Mom said.

Amanda tried the magic word. "Please. Ple-e-e-e-e-e-ease."

It had no effect. As I walked up the sidewalk, she shouted dramatically through her open window, "Goodbye, dear brother!"

Like our house, Gram's house was what Dad called Victorian. Unlike our house, it hadn't fallen on hard times and wasn't constantly under repair.

Gram was like her house—old but in good shape. She was round, with long white hair and surprisingly smooth skin. She always wore gold metal glasses with round lenses (kind of Harry Potter–ish) and long hippie dresses. Oh, and she was a witch.

Gram opened the door before I could get to it.

"How's my favorite grandson?"

I hugged her. I was her only grandson, so I wasn't particularly flattered. I told her I was better than some days but not as good as others, which was what Granddad had always said. My memory of him was kind of vague because he'd died when I was six, but I remembered that.

"How about some hot chocolate or tea?"

"Hot chocolate," I said.

She made hot chocolate for me and tea that smelled like flowers for her. We went into the living room, which had paintings covering most of every wall, some by artists my mother said were now famous. Gram had bought the pieces when the artists were not famous. She had been very "lucky" in her choices. Lucky like Chris and his family.

"So," I said, sitting on her sofa, "you wanted to talk to me?"

"I always want to talk to you," she said.

"Mom made it sound more specific."

"Tell me about this new girlfriend first."

"I don't have a new girlfriend."

"You don't?"

"Not unless I've missed something."

"What day is this?"

I told her.

"What month?"

I told her.

"What year?"

I told her.

"Oops," she said. "Never mind."

I hated it when she did that. Gram could see the future, but she was absentminded about the present and often confused dates.

"When is it supposed to happen?" I asked. "When am I supposed to have a girlfriend?"

"Can't say," she said, pretending to zip her mouth. "You know the rules. Don't want to risk changing the future by giving it away."

"How can you change the future if you can see the future? Isn't it already what it is?"

"Let's change the subject. Tell me about a movie I should see."

I told her about *Edward Scissorhands* (1990; writers: Tim Burton, Caroline Thompson; stars: Johnny Depp, Winona Ryder).

"Sounds lovely," she said when I'd finished describing the plot.

She wouldn't watch it. She never watched movies. She just liked to hear me tell her the plots of movies. She said she loved hearing me talk about something I loved.

Her house was always the right temperature, and the light in the room always just what it should be for the mood I was in. My mood that night was dim, making the room dark and shadowy.

Gram asked me some questions about school and I answered them, and I asked her some questions about her work and she told me about a woman who wanted help training her dog. Unfortunately, the dog had been an emperor in a former life.

"Naturally, he doesn't want to listen to anyone."

"What kind of dog?" I asked.

"Jack Russell," she said.

She'd used several techniques, but the dog resisted her.

"I think I could be dealing with Napoleon. I may need the help of a female Jack Russell. Napoleon had a weakness for the ladies."

SCREENPLAY IDEA: Napoleon the dog is a reincarnation of the conqueror. He is a very small mutt who decides that he will conquer the dog world. He starts with his street, where there are two Labs, a golden, a pit bull, and six miniature poodles. This will comprise the core of his army. Only he has some problems right from the start. The poodles can never remember to call him general. The dogs all keep wanting to take naps. They can be diverted from battle plans by a nice smell from a garbage can.

Gram interrupted my thoughts. She said, "Well, I know you're tired and you have the ride home, so I'll get to the warning."

"I'm getting the feeling this isn't going to be a general warning, like 'Don't smoke.'"

"Afraid not. I'm sorry to say that the girl in your room was not a dead girl."

"You know Amanda saw her. Prodigy Amanda. She thought the girl was dead."

"Your sister is going to be very powerful one day, but she's still a little girl now."

"What did she see, then?"

"I tried reading the tea leaves and also orange juice pulp, which some of the more modern readers claim can be most enlightening, and I came up with a very confusing result. I think the girl who came to your room wasn't dead herself. But something dead—dead and old and very powerful—was controlling her. But here's the really spooky part."

"That wasn't the spooky part?" I said, trying to smile but not pulling it off. "That sounded like the spooky part."

"This old, powerful, and dead something is also alive."

"Alive and dead? Mom said that."

"I wanted to tell you this myself so you would understand that we're dealing with something we don't understand. You're in real danger, Jack."

I finished my hot chocolate like it was a shot of whiskey. It didn't give me the confidence whiskey seems to give guys in movies.

"How old is this old something?"

"Very old. Centuries old."

"What did she want in my bedroom?"

"We have to assume she wanted you. Not in a sexual way, you understand."

"An alive dead person, maybe controlled by someone else, wanted me?"

"When you put it that way, it sounds threatening."

"How would you put it?"

"That sounds about right. Until we get this straightened out, you need to be alert. Do not assume that someone who looks dead is actually dead. Keep your third eye open, Jack."

"My third eye isn't the greatest, you know."

"I'm going to make a trip to the spirit world," she said. "We need to know what exactly we're dealing with."

Back when I was young, Gram used to tell me about the trips she'd taken to the spirit world. But she'd quit going decades ago. Even strong witches needed to make the trips when they were young. It was a very dangerous place.

"You can't," I said.

"I can," she said.

"It's too dangerous."

"I'll be fine. I'll make the preparations. It may take me a few days to get ready."

"This is a bad idea."

"You just keep your third eye open until I've had a chance to go and find out what I can."

"There's got to be a better way."

"We're all in danger. Not just you, Jack. I have to go."

Gram had that look. Unmovable as a mountain.

"Can I at least be your backup?" I said.

"We'll see," she said.

"She did come to my room," I reminded her.

She looked me over, as if she was measuring me. Actually, she was—another talent.

"Did you know you're over six foot now? Just a fraction, but still."

"Tall enough to back you up."

"OK," she said. "You'll be my backup."

I hugged her and said good night. She walked me to the door.

"So am I really going to get a girlfriend?" I said.

She said, "Time will tell," and pushed me out the door.

I rode home. The cold cut right through my jacket. It was silent out on the road, no cars or people, and the doors and windows of the houses were all closed up against the cold. The stars were hard little points of light glittering in the cold sky.

I was plenty worried about the old *something* that wasn't alive or dead or maybe was both, but I couldn't help thinking about my potential girlfriend. Who would she be? For one second I thought of a name I shouldn't: Ash. Stupid. Not possible.

"Not possible," I said to myself. Then I did worse. I answered myself. "You're damn right it's not possible.

She's your friend, and if you want her to stay your friend, you won't think such stupid thoughts."

A dead person crossed the street in front of me. He was translucent and unable to see me—not all dead people could. He was very tall, with a mustache and side-burns. I thought of Gram's warning and tried using my third eye to see if there was anything off about him, but he seemed like a normal enough dead guy to me.

Sometimes when I saw a dead person at night, it made me lonely. I'd think how I'd be that dead person someday. It will be me all alone crossing a street just like him.

"Not Ash," I said again, because the loneliness was making me want something I could never have.

What I needed was a depressing movie. When I was feeling unhappy, watching an unhappy story about unhappy people sometimes cheered me up a little. It helped if things didn't work out in the end. The more depressing, the better.

I thought I might watch *American Beauty* (1999; writer: Alan Ball; stars: Kevin Spacey, Annette Bening, Thora Birch). That one could do it. Then I made a quick list of potential movies to watch. They all had some depressing moments that might brighten my mood.

1. *Old Yeller*
2. *Schindler's List*
3. *Ghost*

Maybe *Braveheart*. That ending especially: William Wallace having his guts torn out as the crowd cheers. Terrible.

I felt better already. A little.

The queen whispers the words and leaves the city. It is dangerous. There are things outside the city that are not human, that roam the night and have enormous power. But this is not her greatest risk. Her greatest risk is that the king will notice she is gone.

The boy waits for her by the river past the second bluff. The moon is full, and she sees his brown face, his long, straight black hair, and the warm eyes so different from her own. Her heart beats harder. How can just seeing him do that to her heart? She knows many things, but she does not know this.

The queen rushes to him. His arms are strong, and she allows herself to feel his strength, so different from her own. Muscle, not magic.

When she kisses the king, his lips are like ice. Each time, she freezes inside. But now, as she kisses the boy, she *feels heat, so much that the back of her neck dampens and her face flushes.*

"I waited," Ishi says. "I worried."

"The king suspects. I have to be careful for both our sakes."

He begs her, as he has many times before, to run away with him. He will leave his tribe, his wife and son (young as he is, he has both), his country, and they will find a new place. He will leave everything for her. Will she leave everything for him?

He does not understand that there is no place to hide. There is no place where the king cannot find them.

As soon as she thinks this, the king finds them.

8

I leaned my bike up against the railing of the stairs to the front porch, trying to remember if *Braveheart* was on instant Netflix. I didn't notice Captain Pike on his porch as I came up the stairs.

"Jack," he said, his voice low and grumbly. As usual, he was smoking a pipe. He liked to smoke his pipe outside on his porch, summer or winter, rain or shine.

Captain Pike had been a captain on riverboats and cargo ships that sailed around the world. He had a glass eye that saw much farther than his natural one — farther even than people with powerful third eyes. He was a hundred and one years old but didn't look a day over seventy-five. Then again, a lot of people in Utopia lived to be over a hundred but looked and acted much younger. They often lied about their age to keep outsiders from getting too interested.

"You're out late," I said. He usually went to bed at about nine o'clock and got up at some crazy time before the sun came up.

"I was asleep," he said. "Something woke me."

"What?" I said.

"My glass eye doesn't sleep, you know. My glass eye woke me."

His glass eye didn't miss much.

"Aye, matey!" I heard Lucy shout from inside the house. Lucy was the captain's parrot and she shouted "Aye, matey!" a lot. She shouted other things, too. She flew all around the house, but Captain Pike never let her outside. He claimed that Lucy had a burning desire to see the moon and she would die trying to fly there.

"What did it see?" I asked. "Your eye."

"Dead girl."

"A dead dead girl?"

"Is there another kind?"

I hadn't thought there was, but Gram seemed to think so, and she knew a lot. More than anyone I knew.

"What dead girl?" I said.

"Died about ten minutes ago. Murdered."

I stared at him. People weren't murdered in Utopia. Ever.

"Are you sure?"

"Up on the Nirvana campus. Probably a student. She's lying on the grass in front of a dorm."

The Captain's pipe bowl glowed orange, and a second later he blew out a cloud of smoke that became the shape of a boat before floating off into the night.

"Maybe she died of natural causes or alcohol poisoning or something," I said.

"Murdered," he said. "But there's something odd about the way it was done. I can't quite see it. Something very odd."

"Should we call someone?" I said.

"The police have already been called."

It was chilly and damp. I saw the dead girl then with my third eye. Just for the flash of a second. She was sprawled on the ground, a crowd gathered around her body.

"Terrible," Captain Pike said. "Murder. Not just this girl, either. I fear there's more to come."

His pipe bowl burned bright orange, and when he blew out this time, the smoke made an image of the Grim Reaper.

He coughed. "Sorry about that," he said.

"I better get to bed," I said. "See you, Captain."

As I walked next door, I remembered the dead girl, the whatever girl, grabbing my heart. I felt something cold all around me. But there was nothing there. Nothing I could see.

9

Amanda woke me up so late I only had time to get dressed and brush my teeth before we had to leave for school. Mom had been called to the Wicked Witch's house early because the Wicked Witch had tripped over one of her minions (she had four fat, wrinkly bulldogs, all named Bruno), so it was up to my alarm and Amanda, both of which had let me down.

I let Amanda ride on the handlebars of my bike, even though it was easier if she just rode behind me on the seat. She was like a dog. She liked the wind in her face.

"Are you picking me up?" she asked when I stopped in front of Thomas Moore Elementary, a square, three-story, red-brick building.

I said Mom would pick her up.

"You better be careful," she said.

"Of what?" I said.

"Cars, dummy," she said. "Look both ways."

She ran toward the school doors. I was relieved she wasn't talking about dead girls who weren't dead girls or live ones. Cars I could handle.

I rode six blocks farther to Utopia High and parked my bike in the rack closest to the south side entrance. On the way to math, I stopped by the bathroom. I was late and hurrying, so naturally a dead girl appeared while I was washing my hands. She was sitting on the window ledge, wearing a short dress, her long pretty legs crossed.

"A little privacy," I said, even though I was just washing my hands.

She had straight blond hair and very dead eyes. No question this one was dead.

"I need," she said. "I need—"

Her expression went blank. I'd seen this happen many times before. The dead tended to lose concentration even easier than we did. ADD is not just for the living.

"I need, I need—"

I considered hurrying on to my class, which was what I should have done. But my gift—or curse, depending on your point of view—made me feel responsible for ghosts. Sometimes a little help from me could turn them in the direction they needed to go in order to move on. That was a good thing. They didn't belong here.

She still looked confused, so I said, "I got that part. *What* do you need?"

"I'm not sure. I can't remember."

"Try."

"I can't. I loved him. I know that."

"Loved who?"

"I loved him," she said. "Real love. I loved him so much I couldn't breathe when he got close."

"You're saying you loved him so much it literally killed you?"

"I loved him," she said, frustrated that I didn't understand. "I loved him. But I'm not sure he loved me. It's terrible not knowing. I need—"

The restroom door swung open and Duke walked in. Duke's real name was Seth. His buddies had given him the nickname Duke because he was big and walked funny (he had a bad knee from football) like John Wayne, whose nickname had also been Duke—though I was surprised and impressed that Seth and his buddies knew this. (For an example of the John Wayne walk, see *True Grit*, 1969; writers: Charles Portis, Marguerite Roberts; stars: John Wayne, Kim Darby, Glen Campbell.)

"Duke," I said.

"Jack," he said, and then looked around nervously. "Cold in here."

The girl had disappeared when Duke came in. Ghosts can be skittish like that.

I hung around until Duke left. I waited for her to come back. I wanted to help her if I could. She seemed lost, one of the lost ones. She didn't reappear, though, and after a few minutes I left.

I found Ash at her locker in the busy hallway and asked her if she'd heard any news about a body being found up at Nirvana College.

"You know I don't listen to the news," she said. "Nothing is ever new."

I saw her boyfriend's snide face in my mind and heard his pompous pronouncement that news was only a highly disguised form of gossip. Of course Ash, being Ash, had adopted the same view.

"Deep," I said. "That sounds like it comes from *Philosophy for Dummies.*"

Her mouth set. "Shut up."

"You always do that," I said. I thought, *Don't say any more. Don't say any more.* But it was like I'd jumped out a window. I couldn't stop until I hit the ground.

"Do what?" she said.

"You become whatever your boyfriend is. You believe what he believes."

"Do I?" she said. Her cheekbones seemed to pop out on her angular face. She pulled a cigarette from her purse and went to light it and then realized she was in the school hallway and stuffed it back in.

Shut up, I thought. *Shut up.*

I named the musician (first got her started in music), the football player (she'd gone to every game and started watching football on TV and joined two fantasy football leagues), the potter (she'd taken a pottery class at Nirvana, studied art online, and taken a trip to Chicago to go to the Chicago art museum—twice). I reminded her of all of them.

"And now the news isn't worth listening to," I said.

We glared at each other.

"So what is the freaking important news?" she asked.

"I think a girl was murdered."

The bell went off.

She stared at me, and I thought she was about to say something. Instead, she gave me a single-finger salute, turned, and strode off. I headed toward my class but made a quick detour into the library to go online and get what news I could.

There was a short "breaking news" piece on the town paper's main site:

A student at Nirvana College was found dead on campus last night. The police were not forthcoming with details, but Channel 7 has learned that the girl's name was Alice Highsmith and that her boyfriend, Brandon Houghton, has confessed to the murder. An argument, heard by other students in the dorm, turned deadly when, allegedly, Ms. Highsmith was shoved by Brandon Houghton and fell through an open window to her death.

I saw a picture of the girl. I recognized her right away: it was the dead girl I'd just seen in the bathroom.

I logged off the computer and hurried on to math. As I sat at my desk watching Mr. Morton write numbers and letters and symbols on the board, I knew I'd have to do something about that dead girl talking about love to me in the boys' bathroom.

"Do you have an answer for us?" Mr. Morton asked.

I was confused at first, but then I saw that the board had a bunch of numbers and symbols on it. I looked down at my blank page.

"Afraid not," I said.

A few snickers.

"Lover boy doesn't like numbers," Dickerson said from behind me.

Bill Wayne added his usual echo, "Lover boy."

Morons. But the morons did make me think about what the dead girl had said: *I loved him. But I'm not sure he loved me.* She must have been talking about her boyfriend, the one who had confessed to pushing her out the window.

She wasn't sure? That seemed an odd thing to say about your killer. Captain Pike had said she was murdered. He didn't say accidently pushed. Something about the dead girl's eyes looked so lost, more lost than any dead person's I'd ever seen. Captain Pike said murder. He wasn't wrong very often.

10

I was late for history class because I was looking for Ash at the smoking wall and then her locker. When I walked in, I saw she was already there but not sitting in her usual place to the left of me in the back row. She was up front with Kiss-Ass Kevin and Jeopardy Julie (nicknames provided by me). She studiously ignored me as I passed. I found a desk next to the Rasta Jock twins.

"Dude," one twin said.

"Dude," the other twin said.

Their voices were exactly the same and they used the same vocabulary. Nathan liked to pretend he was Jason and Jason liked to pretend he was Nathan. Even their parents and their sister couldn't tell them apart, so it always irritated them when I could. Naturally that fact made me take every opportunity to out their identities.

"Jason," I said to the one closest to me. Then I nodded at the other. "Nathan."

"Freak," Jason said.

"Freak," Nathan said.

"We're writing a journal about our day," Jason said. "Pick some character and tell what it's like someplace on a day in 1900. I'm a dying Confederate general. Mr. White assigned it and went for coffee. Looked like he needed it."

"I'm a Union general. I'm also dying. We're brothers. We were one of those families that got split in the Civil War. Brother against brother. Here it is 1900 and we're finally meeting up again in New Orleans."

"He said you can use the book. You can also go to the library if you want. Go online."

"He wants us to feel history."

They shook their heads.

"He lives in the past."

"Sad."

Mr. White strolled in then, carrying a coffee cup with steam rising off it. I coveted his coffee. In spite of the morning's excitement, I was feeling tired.

"Well, look who's decided to grace us with his presence." For someone who could be diverted from a lecture by the mention of Watergate, Mr. White was very aware of attendance. Skewed priorities, I thought. He walked back to my desk. "Someone tell you the assignment?"

"Got it."

"Everything all right?"

His coffee cup came perilously close to my hand. I fought off the urge to reach out and grab it.

"Sure," I said. But thought: *Other than a visit from a dead girl and an argument with my best friend.*

Mr. White nodded and went up to his desk, sipping his coffee as he walked.

I thought for a minute and decided to write my journal from the point of view of Charles Earl Bowles, better known as Black Bart. Black Bart was a stagecoach robber who was afraid of horses so he only robbed stages on foot. He was very polite and never killed anyone. And he left poems at the scenes of some of his crimes. I knew one of them by memory. I think it was written in the 1870s:

I've labored long and hard for bread,
For honor, and for riches,
But on my corns too long you've tread,
You fine-haired sons of bitches.

Granted, most people suspected that Black Bart had died before 1900, but there were rumors that he'd lived in anonymity till 1917. I decided to write about him in a retirement home in San Francisco in 1900. I put my pen to paper, about to write "Black Bart" at the top of the page. But something else came out of my pen instead. Something I didn't and did write.

One night I walked out of my house and down the wide main street of Utopia. A part of me knew I was a dreaming, but another part of me knew I was awake. I saw an angel in the town square. What I saw seemed both impossible and more real than anything I'd ever seen before.

The angel was wearing a white gown. Her skin was pale as moonlight, her hair white. She was like the moonlight itself, luminous.

Her eyes were not human. I felt joy and fear at the same time. It was as if I'd been living my whole life for this moment.

"Joshua Bell," she said. "You are the one."

I saw the shape of her body beneath the white gown. I yearned to touch her, hold her. I felt that if I could just hold her, I would have that thing I had always secretly yearned for but could not name. I never understood myself so well as I did at that moment. But I also felt shame.

She held out her hand.

The shame left me. Thoughts of my wife and children left me. Thoughts of my neighbors and friends and parents and brothers and sisters left me.

None of them mattered.

I took her hand.

• • •

I dropped my pen and read what I'd written. The "I" wasn't Black Bart, and it certainly wasn't me. It wasn't even my handwriting.

I felt the chill of a ghost move through me—move *out* of me, more like. Joshua Bell. She, the angel or whatever, called him Joshua Bell. He was my ancestor, and the founder, along with a wagon train of people he led as wagon master, of Utopia. He disappeared about three years after he founded the town. Just disappeared—no note, no good-byes. There was speculation he'd been taken by Indians or bad men wandering through the territory. Of course, many thought he'd left for some personal reason, though none was ever discovered and his wife went to her dying bed bitterly denying there was one.

If this was his writing—and I thought it was—then had he been inside of me? I felt a little shiver. Ghost walked over my grave, Mom would say. But she would not say, Ghost inside of you writing an assignment *and* not even doing it correctly because Joshua Bell disappeared in 1846. No one would. I'd never heard of anyone having a ghost inside of them.

Get out, I thought, because I was worried he could still be in me. But then I thought, *Right, he'll listen to a stern order to leave.* I added, *please,* thinking it couldn't hurt. Christ, what was happening? I scanned myself with my third eye and felt a little better. No one but me inside me. For now.

• • •

I waited for Ash in the hall after class. She saw me, which was why she walked right past me. This was more than the cold shoulder, more like the cold entire body.

"I'm sorry," I said, trailing after her.

She ignored me for ten steps. Then she spun around. "What is wrong with you?"

"I saw the dead girl," I said, and then added, "And I may be going crazy."

"What are you talking about?" She was still glaring at me, but the intensity was wavering slightly.

"A girl was killed up at Nirvana College. That was the news I was talking about earlier. And I saw her—as a dead girl, I mean. She came to see me in the bathroom. She wants something."

"What does she want?"

"I'm not sure yet."

Ash softened. She knew I struggled with seeing dead people. "Just don't take your dead girls out on me, Bell."

"Sorry."

"Quit saying you're sorry," she said. "Anyway, you were right."

"No, I wasn't." I tried, thinking denial was my best way out, but even I could hear my lack of conviction.

"I mean, I don't change in any essential way, but I do kind of start following my new boyfriend's passions."

"Maybe a little," I said, trying to sound reluctant.

"Right," she said. "A little. At least I have relationships with members of the opposite sex, my celibate friend."

"No one would deny that."

"You know you're an ass."

"I know."

"And you do need a girlfriend, dude. You'd be less cranky."

"Maybe," I said.

"How long has it been since you and Michelle . . . ?"

"A year, I guess."

And what had Michelle Swain said when she was breaking up with me? She liked me but she wasn't going to be any boy's second string. She was a varsity player on both the soccer and volleyball teams, and she thought she should be varsity with the boy she went out with. And what did I say? Nothing.

"Anyway, if seeing dead girls makes you crazy, you've been crazy for as long as I've known you."

True. But dead-not-dead girls. Murdered girls. Invasion of the ancestor. These were new developments. I decided to keep them to myself.

We banged out the doors toward the smoking wall. Blake and Shelby, the drummer in Ash's band, were already smoking by it. Shelby is five feet tall but seems taller because she has this perfect posture. She is two inches too tall to officially qualify as a Little Person, which she claims is the great tragedy of her life.

"All I'm saying," she said as we came up, "is it would make us more unique."

"What would make who more unique?" Ash asked.

"Changing the name of the band," Shelby said.

"That again." Ash rolled her eyes. She was a good eye-roller. She was good at everything. "Changing our name will just confuse our fans."

"What fans?" Shelby asked. "Maybe changing our name will *get us* some fans."

Ash lit a cigarette and added to the substantial cloud of smoke forming by the wall. "Let's ask Jack. He's impartial."

"OK," Shelby said. "How would you like to sleep with me, Jack?"

I wasn't even smoking, but I coughed like smoke had gone down the wrong way.

"Now," Shelby said, "keeping that offer in mind, do you think changing our name from Good Girls with Bad Intentions to Bad Girls with Good Intentions would be a good or a bad idea?"

Ash shook her head sadly at Shelby. "You've corrupted the jury pool. Neither of these boys is any good now. They'll both side with you just on the off chance you'll actually sleep with them."

Shelby looked up at me. "I might actually sleep with Jack."

"Bad Girls," I said. "Good Intentions. Way, way better."

Ash blew smoke in my face. She gave Shelby a second condescending head shake. "Save it for the record producers, Shelby."

Shelby, somehow, stood up even straighter. For a

second she seemed to consider how far she'd have to leap to land on Ash. Then she smiled. "You're just making my point. Bad Girls is more accurate. Let's be real."

"Maybe you're right," Ash admitted. "Maybe we are bad girls. But only some of us have good intentions."

They were both smiling now. Pretty faces and seemingly pretty smiles, but those smiles were like mines buried in gardens. I thought of *The Nightmare Before Christmas* (1993; writers: Tim Burton Michael McDowell; stars: Danny Elfman, Chris Sarandon, Catherine O'Hara) and the ghoulish smiles in that film.

Shelby turned to me. "You and I should go out sometime."

"Sure, yeah, maybe," I babbled, wondering if this was still somehow part of the fight.

"You decide and let me know," she said, and walked off before I could say anything else.

Blake said, "Smooth."

"Since when does she like you so much?" Ash said, as if I'd been holding out on her.

"Does she?"

"You are clueless sometimes," Ash said.

"You better not wait too long or she'll hate you," Blake said.

If you graded by quantity, Blake was pretty much an expert on girls.

"Maybe she was just trying to piss off Ash," I said.

Ash said, "Why would that piss me off?"

I felt disappointed. She flicked her ash. It seemed to require all her attention.

Blake let out a long sigh; luckily he'd already tossed his butt and so had no cigarette smoke to blow in my face. "Who cares why she said it? Go with it, Jack."

"Yeah," Ash said sarcastically. "Just go with it. You can be like Casanova Blake."

"What's wrong with everybody today?" Blake said as Ash stormed off. "Do all of us a favor, dude, and either go for Shelby or go for Ash already."

I *had* gone for Ash once. We'd been having this intense conversation, and I got carried away by the intenseness of the moment and the proximity of our lips (sitting on the sofa, legs and arms touching), and I leaned over and kissed her. At first she kissed me back, but then she jumped up like I'd slipped an ice cube down her shirt. She told me she needed a friend, not another boyfriend. Numerically this was true, but I hoped to defy the numbers. She felt differently. In fact, her words were "I don't need this now. I thought we were friends."

And then she walked out.

So I'd gone for it and I'd gone down in flames.

"Ash and I are just friends," I told Blake. "That's all."

"Yeah," Blake said. "Right. That's all."

The bell rang. Sometimes I thought it would be better for me when Ash went off to Stanford and I wouldn't see her all the time, and sometimes I thought it would be worse — much, much worse.

The king stood about twenty feet away from the queen and Ishi, on a slightly elevated rock that hadn't been there before.

"So this is your short-liver," he said, looking at the boy as he would look at a sheep or slave.

The queen moved in front of Ishi. She could feel he did not like it, feel his muscles tense, his body's urge to rush the king. Next to Ishi, the king looked small and weak. All the same, Ishi would be dead before he took one step if the king felt threatened.

"Kill us both," she said.

The king looked curious. His curiosity made her shake with anger. Ishi had done this, given her the gift—or curse—of feeling.

She hated the king.

"Perhaps I'll wear him, if his appearance pleases you so," the king said.

She knew then that he would. He would torture her with Ishi's body for as long as it lasted. And inside there would be only the king, cold and powerful and untouchable.

She hated him.

11

Most of me didn't want to see the dead girl again, but part of me did. I put off going to the bathroom while most of me wrestled with part of me; I figured the dead girl was most likely to corner me while I was alone, cut off from the herd like a sickly gazelle. If I'd been a girl, I could have just gone up to some other girls and said, "I'm going to the bathroom," and all of them would jump up and say they had to go, too. It was something genetic; girls couldn't let other girls go to the bathroom without them. But if I went up to a group of guys and said, "I'm going to the bathroom," they'd be like, "Why are you telling us, dude? Jesus, go already."

I held my needs in check through my next class, but finally I had to admit defeat, so off I went to the nearest bathroom. Alone.

The dead girl didn't appear until I was washing my hands, which was something to be grateful for, anyway. She was in the mirror this time—literally in the mirror, I realized when I looked over my shoulder and saw she wasn't behind me.

"You've been avoiding me," she said. The dead generally didn't bother with greetings.

"I've been busy," I said.

"I need . . ." she started again, but stopped and looked confused.

This wasn't my first conversation with a dead person. It was best to get one thing clear right from the start: "You do know you're not living anymore, right?"

She glared at me from inside the mirror. "Do you think I'm an idiot?"

"Some people don't know."

She gave me a blank look.

"Sorry about your boyfriend." Still she looked blank. "Pushing you out a window?"

"Brandon didn't push me."

"He says he did."

"He said that?"

"To the police."

"That's a lie."

"You would know, I guess," I said, "but people don't usually confess to murder unless they, you know, murder."

"It's a lie," she said.

"Is Brandon the one you loved? The one you were talking about?"

"Yes. No. I can't remember. Why can't I remember?"

"Death does that sometimes. It clouds the memory."

"Sucks."

"How did you fall out of the window if he didn't push you?"

She made a ghostly moan. I'd never heard one before, except in movies. It was not common among the dead.

Water started spouting out of the faucets, filling the sinks and splashing onto the tile floor. But since the faucets weren't turned on, I couldn't turn them off.

"Not good," I said. "You're leaking. Turn the water off."

"He didn't kill me. He wouldn't. I loved him. He loved me."

"Turn the water off and we'll talk," I said. "Maybe the news was wrong."

"Not right. That's not. He didn't hurt me. He wouldn't." Very agitated voice. The water pressure increased, and one of the faucets shot into the air. Water poured out everywhere.

"There's a reason you can't move on," I said. "Maybe that's it. You don't want to admit he killed you. It's hard, but you have to admit it to move on."

"He didn't kill me."

"You fell. You remember that, right? How did you fall?"

"I can't remember."

Not remembering anything but their death was common among the dead, but they always remembered their death. It was burned in their memory.

"Try," I said.

"I wasn't myself," she said.

Another faucet went flying into the air. The restroom would be a swimming pool before long.

"Turn the water off, Dead Girl, or I'm leaving."

"My name is Alice," she said, but she stopped the water finally. Not soon enough. The bathroom was flooded. I could feel the water soaking through my Converses.

"If you can't remember who killed you, then how can you be sure it wasn't Brandon?"

"We were in love," she said.

"People in love often kill each other." I'd read that somewhere. Most people are killed by people they know. Many by people they love. It was kind of disturbing.

"You're right," she said, which gave me a moment of satisfaction before she added, "I need to know what happened."

"That's not what I meant."

"I need you to go to my dorm room."

"I'm not going to your dorm room."

"Go to my dorm room and get my diary. I need you to tell me what the last entry says. I can't remember, but I think the diary will help me understand."

"I can't," I said.

"Please," she said. "I need to know. You're the only one who can help me."

Unfortunately, this was probably true. Most dead people could only talk to one person like me. Once they talked to one, they couldn't talk to another.

"Please," she said.

Just then I heard the door swing open and the football coach/gym teacher, who we secretly called Bulldog, came though the door.

"OK," I whispered to the dead girl.

She disappeared.

"Jesus H. Christ," Bulldog said, staring at the inch of water on the floor.

"I didn't do this," I said.

"Your ass is mine, Bell," he growled.

I thought about trying to defend myself—maybe blaming faulty school plumbing—but his bulldog face was swollen and bright red and he looked close to taking a bite out of me.

SCREENPLAY IDEA: Steroid-addled gym teacher goes on a killing rampage at a local high school when an innocent boy stupidly talks back. He drowns his victims in school bathroom sinks. No, in toilets. He leaves behind a football at every murder. When the cops finally catch him, he says, "I could have been a pro football player, you know. I just could never remember the snap count. Fucking snap count."

• • •

Principal Thompson was not happy to see me again so soon. I wasn't happy to see him, either, but unlike him, I wasn't rude enough to say so directly.

"I'm very disappointed to see you so soon, Jack," he said.

"I can't help it if the plumbing went crazy," I said. I turned to Bulldog. "Did you actually see me turn on the faucets?"

"Do something this time, Paul," Bulldog growled. "This kid is out of control." He marched out of the office.

Principal Thompson shut his door and motioned for me to take a seat.

"Things just seem to have a way of happening around you," he said with unusual sarcasm.

"Thank you for understanding."

He sat down in his comfortable office chair and sighed heavily. He leaned back a little.

"Tell me what happened," he said. "Tell me how you did it."

He tried to sneak that last sentence in, but his interrogation techniques needed work. For the next fifteen minutes, he tried to trip me up. It was like he'd recently binged on TV cop shows, but I just kept telling him what was essentially the truth: The water just started flowing out. I had nothing to do with it.

"You're saying you didn't turn the water on, flood the

bathroom, and turn off the faucets right before Bull—I mean Mr. Sheldon—came in?"

"Check the security footage," I said. "You'll see."

He sighed again. That sighing was not a good habit in a principal. "You know we don't have security cameras in the bathrooms."

"Probably would upset some parents," I said. "So what you're saying is you have no proof it was me. It could have been anyone. Or it could have just happened. You know how it is around here. Sometimes things just happen."

He cleared his throat. He did know how it was, but he did his best to pretend he didn't.

"I don't want to see you again, Jack. Not for a while. Stay out of trouble. Keep your nose clean."

That expression always confused me, but I didn't say anything about it. Instead I said, "Yes, sir," because I wanted to get out of there.

The "sir" seemed to do the job. He told me to leave. I opened the door and breathed the fresh air of freedom— except that it was more a smell of coffee and sweet perfume, thanks to Mrs. Sandhill, administrative assistant.

There was a moment of elation at escaping Principal Thompson's office, but it was squashed when I remembered what I'd agreed to do before Bulldog showed up: I'd agreed to go to a murdered girl's dorm room and search for a diary.

12

After school I skipped detention again. I felt bad about it but not so bad I didn't skip. I rode my bike over to the Nirvana campus, which was about six blocks away. There was no denying that it was a beautiful campus: old stone and brick buildings with ivy growing up them, big elms and oaks and white birches dotting the wide, lazy lawns. It was a rich school with students who came from rich families, or at least very well-off ones. People with "more money than sense," as Gram described them.

I'd been to a few lectures at the college, which were often open to the public. I went to one by this really famous medium named Henry Henry. He was very convincing if you knew nothing about dead people. He had this totally deep, powerful voice and he told awesome stories. But he also had a dead guy standing right next to him the whole time and he never even noticed him. Sort of undermined his credibility in my eyes.

The only other place I'd been on campus was the student union. I went there to watch football games sometimes on their massive-screen TV. The coed dorm was next to the student union. I didn't know if Alice had lived there, but I hoped so because I'd have a harder time getting into the girls' dorm.

I passed a statue of a blue goddess with about ten arms. She was sitting cross-legged and was adorned with anklets and bracelets. Something about her was kind of attractive, which was disturbing.

SCREENPLAY IDEA: A multi-armed goddess shows up in a small town much like Utopia. She's blue, but she's got a hot body and is hot in many other ways, including her ability to breathe fire. She's a goddess and all, but she's kind of lonely. She meets this guy who works at the public library and is a college student. His name is Sam. They fall in love. They have some pretty hot sex. All those arms. But then the multi-armed goddess's dad turns up and there's big trouble. He hates humans. And Sam's parents, it turns out, hate multi-armed blue goddesses. (Note: Romantic comedy / horror / supernatural thriller. A festival movie or summer blockbuster?)

• • •

The door to the dorm wasn't locked and there was no guard, but I saw the charms over the door and I worried they might be there to detect intruders. I used my third eye to try to see how strong they were. I didn't see anything, which at first I assumed was my limited abilities—my third eye being somewhat unreliable, particularly when I tried to force it to show me things. But then I realized I didn't see anything because there was nothing to see; these charms were the kittens of charms. Pitiful. The air got a little thicker when I walked through the door. That was all I felt from them.

I realized that Alice hadn't given me her dorm room number, which was just like dead girls. Very forgetful. I'd just have to walk the halls until I found the yellow crime scene tape that was always over a door where a crime had been committed. (See about a million movies, including, for example, *Goodfellas*, 1990; writers: Nicholas Pileggi, Martin Scorsese; stars: Robert De Niro, Ray Liotta, Joe Pesci.) People who said you couldn't learn anything from movies were daft, which was a word I'd learned from British movies—further proof of my point.

There was nothing on the first floor except way too many open doors with people inside them meditating in the lotus position. Ditto the second floor. The strong stench of incense drifted from the rooms out into the hall.

I opened the door from the stairway to the third and final floor. A few steps in, I saw yellow tape over the doorway of an open door. It made an X. I strolled by, fake whistling (I know, stupid, but I was nervous), and casually glanced in and saw two men: a gaunt bearded guy with black-framed glasses who had the look of a Nirvana College professor and a middle-aged guy, fit, with the thickest eyebrows I'd ever seen, who I was pretty sure was a detective.

I loitered just beyond the door and tried to listen. It wasn't hard. They were talking loudly.

"Look, Professor, you called me. The boy has confessed. Love triangle. You said you had something to tell me. So tell me. I'm here."

"It was an accident," the professor said. "He didn't mean to kill her."

"Is that right?"

"That's right."

"That's interesting. Real interesting. So you must have some proof of this to give me. That must be why you called me here. 'Cause you know what time it is?"

The professor sounded uncertain: "I'm afraid I don't."

"Cocktail hour. It's almost time for the cocktail hour."

"I'm afraid I don't drink."

"That's too bad. Better give me your proof, then."

"I saw what happened in a dream. The boy pushed her, but it was an accident. He didn't mean to kill her."

"A dream?" the detective said. Flat. Sarcastic. He reminded me of Tommy Lee Jones in *The Fugitive* (1993; writers: David Twohy, Jeb Stuart; stars: Harrison Ford, Tommy Lee Jones).

"I see things. I'm gifted. So there's your proof. He did not mean to kill her. If you need me to testify, I will."

"A dream, Professor? Tell you what. Let's put our cards on the table. Did someone see something and come to you?"

"The dream was very clear," the professor said. "The boy didn't intend to kill her."

"Dreams don't mean a whole lot in court."

"They should," the professor said.

I could hear the frustration in the detective's silence. He knew the man was lying, but he didn't know how to force the professor to tell him what he wasn't telling him.

My eavesdropping was interrupted by a voice behind me that whispered, "What do you think you're doing?"

I turned. At first I thought it was Alice, because the girl was willowy and blond, but it was a different willowy blond girl. There were a lot of them attending Nirvana College.

"Listening," I whispered back.

"Why?"

I decided to tell the truth: "Alice told me to."

"My dead roommate Alice?" she said.

"Yes."

"Oh," she said. Then she gave me the standard Nirvana student greeting: "*Namaste*. Don't do drugs. Life is magic," which had been coined by His Holiness, the Cowboy Guru.

"Sure," I said. "*Namaste* to you, too."

"You'd better follow me." The girl opened a door across the hall, and I followed her into a small room that looked pretty much like all the other small dorm rooms I'd caught sight of. She shut the door behind us.

Colorful pictures of gods and goddesses (some with multiple arms and heads) were on the wall. Incense burned on a night table. It was very tidy; everything seemed to be where it should be. So why did it feel like something was wrong here? Like something was out of place?

"I'm Harmony, Alice's roommate," the girl said. "Alice's former roommate, I mean. I'm staying over here because they won't let me stay in our room. God, I still can't believe it. I've been trying to contact Alice, but I haven't been able to."

She paused and looked at me with suspicion. "Why is she talking to you? Who are you?"

"No one."

"Did you even know her?"

I shook my head.

"I was her best friend. She *should* talk to me."

"I see dead people," I said. I tried to sound like the kid in *The Sixth Sense*. It was kind of my line. "Hear them. Sometimes even accidentally walk through them. You don't."

She seemed about to deny this but changed her mind.

"Did she say anything to you about me?"

"No," I said. "Like what?"

"Nothing," she said. "It's terrible. The way she died. I can't believe she's really gone."

"Who are the men in your room?"

"One's a detective. The other is a professor. He claims he sees things in dreams with a third eye, but he's just another fraud. I came here expecting to meet all kinds of talented people, but most of them don't have any talent at all. You do, though. I can see you're not lying. You really do." She was looking at me closely again, like maybe she was trying to see my aura or something.

"Alice is confused," I said. "She thinks her boyfriend didn't kill her."

"Brandon didn't," Harmony said.

"How do you know?"

"He wouldn't."

"They were arguing," I said. "The detective said there was a love triangle."

She looked away. I thought I saw a slight flush to her cheeks.

"People argue. But Brandon wouldn't hurt a fly. Literally." She went into his humane behavior toward flies. He must have been a saint in the fly world.

"The professor claimed he saw it all in a dream," I said. "He saw Brandon push her."

"I told you, Dr. Weingarde is a fake. Brandon wouldn't. He wasn't a violent person. He isn't a violent person."

"Which brings up the kind of obvious question," I said. "Why did Brandon confess if he didn't do it?"

"I don't know," Harmony said, shaking her head. "I haven't talked to him since last night. But I know he couldn't kill her."

"Then why say he did?" I was doing my best to question the girl using my vast experience with detectives in films — Sherlock Holmes, Sam Spade, Rick Deckard, Clarice Starling, Veronica Mars, The Dude.

"Maybe someone asked him to?"

"Who?"

"I don't know," she said, which I thought was probably a lie.

"Why, then?"

She turned away. I could feel her pulling back from me. "I don't know what happened. Alice had been acting so strange lately. Really strange. It was almost like she was, you know, schizophrenic or something. Like she wasn't herself. Anything could have happened. I just know Brandon didn't kill her."

"How was she not herself?" I said. People always lied to detectives in films. Example: Sam Spade in *The Maltese Falcon* (1941; writers: John Huston, Dashiell Hammett; stars: Humphrey Bogart, Mary Astor).

"She was disconnected. She said odd things. She didn't care about the things she'd always cared about."

"What about Brandon? Was he acting strange, too?"

She shook her head. "He was freaked out by her. We both were."

"Where were you when she was killed?"

"Not here. I wish I had been. I was with a friend."

"She was your friend, right? Best friend?"

"I wasn't here."

"Too bad." Who was I channeling then? A dozen untrusting movies detectives from a dozen different movies.

"Did Alice tell you to ask me all these questions?"

"She can't remember what happened," I said. "She wants to."

"I can't help you. I wish I could."

"She needs your help."

"I can't help her or you," she said. She opened the door and motioned me out.

I walked down the hall past Alice's room in case the detective and professor were gone and I'd have the chance to look for the diary. That was a mistake. Both the detective and the professor looked right at me as I paused to look in.

"Excuse me," the detective said.

I pretended not to hear him and walked on and was almost to the stairway exit when the detective came out of the room.

"Hold on there," he ordered.

I don't know why I had such a problem with authority. It really was bound to get me in trouble someday. I took off running. I'd seen enough movies to know that law-enforcement officials were kind of like dogs. If someone ran, the cops chased. So—stupid. But once I'd started running, I couldn't stop. I banged through the hall door and took the stairs two at a time.

The detective was fast, faster than I was. It was just my luck that I'd get a track-star cop. He'd almost caught up to me by the time I got to my bike. Fortunately, I hadn't locked it (breaking one of the Bell family rules of property protection). I jumped on and took off. I could hear the detective's sharp breaths as I pedaled. He was that close. His hand brushed against the back of my neck, but by then I was gaining some speed and he wasn't able to keep up. He made one final grab for me and missed.

I cut across campus and down to the river and only slowed when I was sure he wasn't trying to cut me off or something. I had a feeling he would go back and talk to Harmony. I had just made myself, as they say on cop shows, "a person of interest."

Stupid. Stupid. Stupid.

I followed the river until I came to Ponder Road and cut up to my neighborhood. Alice appeared as I turned down my street. I braked and skidded sideways into and through her.

"That does not feel good," she said, looking down at her translucent body as I went through.

An extreme cold, so cold it was almost hot, passed through me.

"It wasn't good for me, either," I said when I'd stopped.

She was in front of me then. The dead moved outrageously fast.

"Did you get the diary?" she said.

"I couldn't get in. There was a detective in the room."

"Going through my things?"

"Talking to a professor. Dr. Weingarde."

Alice frowned.

"I talked to your friend Harmony."

"I don't want to talk about her."

"Why is that?"

"She's not my friend."

"What did she do?"

"I don't remember." This time I thought she might be lying. Lies from the living. Lies from the dead.

She started to fade.

"What did she do, Alice?"

"I need to see my diary," she whispered as she faded into the air. A second later, she was gone.

13

I shouted hello when I came into the house, and my mom shouted hello back from what sounded like the kitchen. No hello from Amanda or my dad. I went up to my room, keeping my eyes open for would-be attacks from my would-be attacker.

At the same time I was thinking about Alice and her boyfriend and her roommate.

> **SCREENPLAY IDEA:** A girl murders her roommate and frames her roommate's boyfriend because the three of them have a secret.

What was the secret, though? It would have to be something good.

They made a pact with the devil.

No.

They cheated on a chemistry exam.

No.

They bet on dog races and now they owed the Russian mob money they didn't have, but the girl, who happened to be her roommate's beneficiary, would get money from an insurance policy.

Definitely no.

Apparently the secret was a secret to me.

I went into the bathroom and splashed water on my face. I heard a giggle just before Amanda jumped from behind the shower curtain and onto my back, a feat she accomplished by climbing onto the toilet lid, which, per Mom's regulations, was down.

"Got you!" she shouted as I spun around and nearly lost my balance.

She began to scream as I turned in circles; the screaming was mixed with giggling. We spun out into the hallway, and then I went down on my knees so I could gently remove her. She saw the end was near and slid off.

"I got you," she repeated.

"Yes, you did."

"You need to be more alert."

"You're probably right."

"Now you have to watch TV with me."

"Can't. I have an important business meeting in the bathroom."

"No, you don't."

I got up and went toward the bathroom, and she jumped up. I slipped in and locked the door behind me. Until Cato learned to pick locks, I was safe.

At dinner that night, Dad was reading the Iowa City paper. There was a story about Alice in it and a picture of her. She was a lot prettier in the picture than she was dead, but I suppose that was true of most people.

"I saw that dead girl," Dad said. "Beautiful girl."

Dad didn't have the family gift—or curse, depending on your point of view—so this confused me.

"You saw her?" I said.

"At the Harvest Festival Parade. She was Corn Queen."

"Last summer?" I said.

He nodded. "She was so beautiful."

"Nineteen," Mom said. "According to the paper, she was nineteen."

"She was probably the prettiest Corn Queen they'd ever had," he said. "The girl was flawless."

"No one is flawless," Mom said, her voice flat and threatening, like the drone of a heart-rate monitor when a heart's stopped beating.

"She was a beautiful girl," Dad said. "That's all I was saying."

"That's all you were saying," Mom said.

"Yes," he said.

"She was nineteen."

"Claire."

"And she's dead. Murdered, from what I read. But yes, let's all focus on how beautiful she was. The prettiest Corn Queen they've ever had."

"Come on, Claire. I didn't mean anything."

"I know you didn't," she said, "but I just can't listen to you not mean anything in that way anymore."

She pushed her chair back and walked out of the room. We watched her. It was like an earthquake, something completely unnatural in our house, tearing it apart.

"What's going on?" I asked Dad.

"'Notice that the stiffest tree is most easily cracked, while the bamboo or willow survives by bending with the wind.' Your mother and I are like the willow."

I would have said Bruce Lee, though it might have been Gandhi. Definitely not Jack Kerouac. Jack was not a bender with the wind. I didn't guess, though. Amanda didn't, either. We were scared. Amanda felt what I did on some level. Mom never, ever walked away from the dinner table. Until now.

"Aren't you going to go after her?" I said to Dad.

He sighed. "I always do, don't I? Not this time, though. This time I'm going to my bar and I'm going to have a drink."

He got up stiffly and walked right out of the house. Amanda and I sat at the dinner table, both in shock. Our parents weren't acting like our parents.

"Are they getting a divorce?" Amanda said.

"No," I said. "Of course not."

Then I googled divorce rates on my phone. Fifty percent. Not good.

"We've got to stop them," Amanda said.

"How?"

"We won't be bad anymore," she said. "We'll be so good they won't ever get angry."

"It's not about you or me, Amanda."

"We both have to be so good," she repeated. "Better than ever. I'm going to get up the first time Mom asks. I'm going to make my own breakfast. I won't ask for any presents for Christmas."

This made me sad. Amanda loves Christmas.

I wanted to promise her they weren't getting a divorce, but I couldn't. I was scared, too. It was the slow kind of scared, something rising, like when the river swells in a flood. First it goes over the banks and then it spreads and spreads until it covers everything and people find themselves on the roofs of their houses, stranded. Sometimes something you never thought would happen, happens.

"It's between them" was all I could think to say.

Between them. When we drove off to the West Coast three summers ago, Dad was being Mr. Tour Guide and pointing to this place or that place where Sal Paradise, the main character of *On the Road,* had stopped. We were in the big old Chevy with the big seats and wide windows. And he reminded us for the thousandth time that Jack Kerouac had said the best apple pie à la mode was in Des Moines, Iowa. And my mother finally was too irritated to keep quiet. She said, "It's not the Bible. It's not *War and Peace* or *Moby-Dick.* You need to read more books, honey pie."

And my father said, "I love you, Claire, but I'm a simple man. I don't see dead people. I'm never going to read *War and Peace* or *Moby-Dick. On the Road* reminds me what it's like to be young every time I read it."

She leaned over and kissed him and everything was solved.

I couldn't imagine Mom without Dad, or Dad without Mom. They loved each other. If they couldn't stay together, no one could.

14

That night I saw Alice in a dream, only she wasn't dead. She was in a parade, waving from a float that was in the shape of an ear of corn. People were crowded along Divine Drive, which is one of the main streets in town. I was in the crowd and then I was next to her on the float and she whispered in my ear, "I love him so much. Loved him. Love him. I can't leave until I know. I can't."

Blood started pouring out of her mouth and all over her sparkly gown. I put my hand over her mouth, but then blood spilled out of her nose and her ears. It streamed down my arms and soaked her white gown until it became red. So much blood. It splashed into my face, my eyes.

"Love isn't being crazy," she said. "Love is being saner than you've ever been. I wasn't crazy, Jack."

She went limp, and the blood flowed off the float and filled the street, like a flooding river, washing everyone in town away, drowning them in blood.

I woke drenched in blood — or what I thought was blood but then realized was sweat — breathing hard and sharp and everything feeling wrong. I sat up and turned on the light.

Love is being saner than you've ever been.

It was late, but I texted Ash. I didn't expect her to text back until the morning.

I lay my phone down. A second later I heard the *ping* and picked it back up.

OK.

I'd written **I need your help.**

Her answer: **OK.** No questions. Just **OK.**

I smiled. I turned the light off.

The king calculates. He is strong, but the queen is strong, too. She cannot defeat him, but she can hurt him, maybe hurt him badly. She could show the others that he is not invincible. He is vulnerable. Yes, he is incredibly powerful, but he is not invincible. He knows he has a weakness. He needs bodies to keep living.

"I could kill you both," he says. "Or I could wear the short-liver and force you to see him every time you see me."

The queen waits. She knows the king and she waits.

"Or I could let you live," he says.

"But," she says. A condition or the false smile? A false smile means death.

"Perhaps we can make a bargain," he says.

"What kind of bargain?"

"I will let you live, but not in this universe."

"Both of us?"

And there is the false smile. "Both of you."

15

The next morning Mom and Dad didn't fight. It was worse. They were polite. *Very* polite.

"Please pass the sugar."

"Here you go."

"Thank you."

"You're welcome."

Mom didn't make fun of Dad once and he didn't make fun of her. Amanda and I watched it all like we were watching a horror movie. (See *Night of the Living Dead*, 1968; writers: George A. Romero, John A. Russo; stars: Duane Jones, Judith O'Dea, Karl Hardman.)

After breakfast I told Mom about what Gram was planning, her walk to the spirit world and all. I should have told her sooner, but I'd been distracted by her and Dad fighting.

"You should have told me sooner."

"She said it would take her a few days to get ready. And she said I could be her backup."

"Don't be ridiculous," Mom said. "If she goes, and I don't think she should, you won't be anywhere near. This is dangerous."

"That's why she needs me."

"She's too old for this. Just—just let me handle her, Jack."

She got that look on her face: end of discussion. I let her think it was.

I gave Amanda a ride to Thomas Moore Elementary on the handlebars of my bike. She was unusually quiet. When I let her off, she said, "I'm scared, Jack. Are you scared?"

"It's going to be OK," I said.

"How will it be OK?"

"They'll figure it out. They love each other. They will never not love each other."

"Pinkie promise?" she said.

So I stuck out my pinkie, and she wrapped hers around mine and then bumped into me and gave me a fierce hug and ran up to school.

Before class I did two things. I called Gram to check on her progress in getting ready for the spirit world, but she didn't answer. Then I went to the smoking wall to see Ash because I had a flash third-eye image that she was there catching a quick smoke before first period. She was.

"I think I'm going to quit," she announced.

I'd been telling her she should quit since we were freshmen, but hearing this now, when everything seemed to be changing, was strangely disconcerting. I almost told her that now was not the time to give up cigarettes. But I caught myself.

"You should," I said.

"So what do you need my help with?"

"Getting something."

"Getting what?"

"Nothing much. Just a diary."

"Sounds easy," she said, and blew smoke in my face because she wasn't the least bit stupid.

"OK. Maybe it's not that easy, but it is just a diary."

"Is it really heavy?"

"No."

"Then I have to ask why you'd need me."

"Moral support?" I said.

"It's in a place where it's hard to get, isn't it?"

"It's just a matter of you watching, being the lookout."

"Whose diary?"

"A girl's."

"The dead girl you've been seeing?" she said. "The one from Nirvana College?"

"She was the Corn Queen," I said, trying to distract her.

"Really?" she said, not impressed.

"My father saw her at the parade last year. We were eating dinner last night, and he said she was the most beautiful Corn Queen he'd ever seen."

"He said that in front of your mom?" Her tone was sharp.

"Yeah. She was really mad at him about it, too."

"Imagine that."

"I don't have to. I saw it."

"You're so observant about me and my boyfriends. No idea why your mom might be upset?"

"Not really."

"I guess your mom never told you who the Corn Queen was in 1993."

She blew smoke at me. I really wished I smoked; I wanted nothing more than to blow smoke back at her right now.

"She was?"

"Good guess," she said.

"How do you know that?"

Ash ignored the question. "Your mother is beautiful."

"I know."

"You ever tell her?"

"Maybe."

She gave me a scornful look. I felt a tickle of guilt like the scratchy beginning of a sore throat.

She waited for me to say something more, and when I didn't, she dropped her cigarette butt and squashed it under her boot.

"When do you want to steal the dead girl's diary?" she asked.

"Tonight."

"Come by and get me, then. Borrow your mom's car. I don't want to have to ride on the back of your bike."

"I'd let you ride on the handlebars like Amanda," I said.

"Pass."

The bell went off and we walked back up to school.

16

In English, Mr. Van Horn read us the whole first chapter of *The Great Gatsby*. It was twenty-four pages in my edition. Why he decided to read the whole thing when he'd already assigned it as homework, I didn't know, but I was grateful because I hadn't had time to (re)read it. At the same time, it made me a little sad and it—for some reason—made me think of my parents' coldness toward each other. That last paragraph especially made me sad. Gatsby standing out on a dock by himself at night. Nick watching him from across the water, thinking he could see him tremble. The tiny green light on the end of the dock. It was all so lonely.

I think it made me sad because I knew how the novel ended. And I worried that my mom and dad's love might be in danger of a bad ending, too.

A lot of teachers would have ruined it by asking us what that green light symbolized, but Mr. Van Horn didn't. He just asked us how it made us feel. One girl said afraid. One girl said helpless and small. One guy said hopeful.

"But it's just a little green light," Mr. Van Horn said.

"But it's more, too," someone said. "It's where Daisy lives, right?"

"It's where he thinks she lives," someone else said.

We argued about this but then decided it didn't really matter if she lived there or not. He saw that light and it made him closer to her, made him remember her and want her all over again.

"This is a story about romantic love, among other things," Mr. Van Horn said. "The author makes us feel Gatsby's desire for something that isn't named with that little scene. We don't need to know what it is yet. We just need to feel it in our bones. But we also feel that the something is dangerous."

"But what are you saying?" Robin said. "What does that green light stand for, Mr. Van Horn? I mean, what do you want us to write down in our notes?"

"I think we've already established that it could stand for a lot of things. What do you think it stands for?"

"I don't know," she said. "A lot of things, I guess. But what one thing do you want us to remember about it?"

Robin was a straight-A student. She liked teachers to

tell her what to remember and then she remembered it. That was how she got all those As.

"Whatever you want to remember. Just tell me how it makes you feel and how it makes Gatsby feel. Try to explain it in greater detail as you have more context, more of the story. Maybe your feelings will change."

"Change? My feelings for what? I need information, Mr. Van Horn. All you did was read to us."

"That's true," he said. "OK. That's all for today. Take off."

Everyone except for Robin made a run for the door. She sat at her desk, looking resentful. I had a feeling Mr. Van Horn was about to hear about that resentment.

After classes I served my detention with the librarian, Mrs. Archer. I tried to convince her to let me off the last four-fifths of my detention based on good behavior, which seemed a fair request given the fact that prisoners in our prison system, whose crimes were a thousand times more severe than mine—armed robbery and assault with a deadly weapon and things like that—often served only a third of their sentences. And if school was teaching us the ways of the real world, shouldn't we detention students only serve part of our sentences?

"If you would just apply this much thinking to your classes, you would be a straight-A student like your mother was," Mrs. Archer said.

I hadn't really thought about it, but Mrs. Archer was about the same age as my parents.

"You knew my mom back in the day?"

"We were in the same class."

"And my dad?"

"I didn't really know him much, but your mom and I were friendly. She was a very good student. Your dad not so much. He could have been, but he was . . . Well, he applied his talents to areas other than school."

I saw my dad then, with my third eye. He was closing up Field of Dreams for the afternoon, but a pretty woman was still sitting at a table talking to him while he cleaned up. They were just talking, but she seemed a little too friendly. I turned away from the image.

"They still got together somehow," I said, but I couldn't help thinking that they had, that morning at breakfast, seemed further apart than I'd ever seen them.

"Yes, they did. They were both rebels in a way. Your mom was a good student and involved in things, but the way she thought, what she said—she wasn't conventional. Your dad was cool, more of the rebel without a cause. They fit somehow."

They fit. That was right.

Still, their dreams hadn't come true. My dad wasn't traveling the world and writing down his adventures, and my mom wasn't teaching English in a college or a university. She'd gotten her bachelor's degree at the University of Iowa. My dad had traveled around the country for two years and then come back to Iowa and enrolled part-time at the U of I. He'd lasted two years. They married in Iowa City but moved back to Utopia when Mom graduated. They'd been here ever since.

And now Dad was talking to strange women in his bar and Mom was leaving rooms because she couldn't stand talking to him. I don't know. They should have been more somehow.

After detention, I called my mom and said I was going to be late for dinner because I was stopping by Blake's to talk about a school project, but really what I was doing was going to the movies, which was where I often went when I was feeling low. We had only one theater in town, so that was the one I went to. It was called Goodfellow's Chinese Theater after a famous theater in Hollywood and Mr. Goodfellow, the owner. It had a red tin roof meant to look like the roof of a Chinese temple over the marquee. Inside, everything was bright red: red walls with classic movie posters on them, a red carpet, glass cases filled with jade figures on — you guessed it — red velvet. Huge paper lanterns hung from the ceiling, and several life-size woodcuts of bald-headed Chinese monks were scattered around the room.

Mr. Goodfellow liked to call himself Irish Chinese. Though he was a white guy of Irish descent, he claimed to have a Chinese soul. Mr. Goodfellow's gift — or curse, depending on your point of view—was that he could visit distant places with his mind. He had been to China and many, many other places without ever leaving Utopia.

My dad didn't approve. He thought people should have to travel to travel.

"Don't get me wrong," he'd say. "It's an awesome ability, but you miss the emotional connection. I mean, part of what means so much to me about those days I spent on the road was the random hardships I overcame, like struggling to find a safe bush to sleep under in LA or having that guy in Deming, New Mexico, pull a gun on me. Goodfellow can't really enter lives just observing."

My mom told me not to be too late. That was her response to my saying Blake and I were doing a school project together? It was a lame lie. Blake's idea of a school project was seducing a girl at a football game. Normally my mom would have been all over the lie. She would have asked me something like "How will you make it as a screenwriter if you don't try harder to make your lies more believable?" Instead I got "Don't be too late." It was discouraging.

One of the things I loved most about our movie theater, though there were plenty who complained about it, was that Mr. Goodfellow changed the movies at random. He'd play new releases for a few weeks, but sometimes he'd play a classic for a day or two. The only way you'd know what was playing was to look at the marquee and the posters in the glass cases next to the doors. I preferred to be surprised, so I didn't look. Instead I rode around back to the alley and locked my bike to a metal ladder that went up the side of a two-story building. Then I climbed the ladder all the way to the roof.

It was a nice view. I could see the river and bluffs to the north and the flat farmland to the south. Where else was I going to get a view like this? And there was no other theater like Mr. Goodfellow's anywhere, either. When I thought of leaving, I thought of all the little things I'd miss. There were a lot of them.

My next act I called "jumping between tall buildings in a single bound." Actually, there was only about a yard between the building I was on and the theater roof, but the long drop to the ground and the hard concrete below magnified those three feet in my mind. I walked back about ten feet and ran to the end of the roof and long-jumped the space between and landed a good distance past the edge. There was a heavy metal hatch at the center of the theater's flat roof, and I squatted to lift it. I started climbing down another metal ladder, but two rungs down, I had to close the hatch above me, which meant going down the rest of the way in pitch-black.

Voices boomed at me because I was behind the screen and the echo back there was deafening. I could tell it was still just the trailers.

The last part was the trickiest because I had to come through the velvet curtains to the front row. If Mr. Jenkins, the manager, was working, he'd be watching for me. He hated me. Unfortunately for him, I was a lot quicker than he was and he seldom caught me. Only twice in all the years I'd been sneaking in. Both times he called the police.

I got arrested pretty often, but my crimes weren't going to get me on anyone's most-wanted list. Stuff like sneaking into the theater. One underage drinking charge (for one lousy beer!). Kidnapping Bulldog's bulldog and dyeing him pink (I forgot to mention this additional reason Bulldog didn't like me much). My mom or dad had had to come and pick me up from the police station way too many times. Mom liked to ask me if I really wanted to be a petty criminal.

"I wouldn't mind so much if you robbed a bank or held up an armored car, but this little stuff is just irritating."

She wasn't fooling me. I knew she was using some kind of reverse psychology. Still, it's kind of disconcerting to have your mother advise you to hold up a bank.

I found a seat in the first row right as the last preview ended. Perfect timing. I loved this part. The start of a movie — the lion's roar or whatever first image introduced the start of a film. Then the opening credits and music. There was something so hopeful about the beginning of a movie. It was like being a kid and opening presents early Christmas morning when it was still dark outside. And I loved sitting in the dark of the theater, the big screen filling up a whole wall. I loved the smell of buttery popcorn, whether I was eating any or not.

The movie turned out to be *Harry Potter and the Deathly Hallows Part II* (2011; writers: Steve Kloves, J. K. Rowling; stars: Daniel Radcliffe, Emma Watson, Rupert Grint), which I'd seen before. I would give it four out of five stars because I loved the books and story so much, but great filmmaking it wasn't.

I was considering whether four stars was too high and didn't hear someone come up from behind me until the seat next to me squeaked. I swung around, ready to run the opposite way. Luckily, it wasn't Mr. Jenkins; it was Mr. Goodfellow, the owner. He was wearing a red Chinese silk robe with jade buttons and some kind of black slippers.

"He's not on duty today, Jack," he said.

Mr. Goodfellow knew how I got into the theater, but he didn't care. In fact, he seemed to enjoy Mr. Jenkins's frustration, which was pretty awesome for me. Mr. Jenkins didn't know about the roof hatch and never could figure out how I got in. He'd even gone so far as to have the back exit door replaced to keep me out.

"Until Jenkins can figure it out," Mr. Goodfellow had told me once, "you can come and go as you please."

When Mr. Goodfellow caught me, he never called the police. He always let me watch the movie. That day we watched it together. There were only a few customers, so it felt almost like a private screening. He even got us popcorn at one point. After the movie was over, I walked out the front with him.

"Been anywhere good lately?" I asked him.

"Cairo. What a wonderful city. Full of past mysteries." Mr. Goodfellow gave me a deep bow and a Chinese fortune cookie from a glass bowl by the entrance when I left.

I tore open the cellophane wrapper as I circled around the block to where I'd left my bike. The fortunes were notoriously accurate, especially if Mr. Goodfellow handed them to you. This one said: SOMEONE WANTS TO MEET YOU. EXPECT AN UNEXPECTED VISITOR.

17

I went home and Amanda didn't even try her Cato attack on me. She was sitting in the living room watching an animated movie, something very girly with little princesses and stuff. I said hello and she said hello back and ordered me to come and watch TV with her. I respectfully declined, though seeing her sitting on the sofa looking small and lonely almost convinced me to, in spite of the obvious torture it would be.

"Maybe later," I said.

Mom and Dad were in the kitchen at the table, but they weren't talking. They were looking at their hands.

"Home from another day of educational enlightenment," I said, planning to back out of the room.

They didn't give me the chance.

"Come and sit down," Dad said.

"Dinner's ready," Mom said. "We were just waiting for you."

None of the usual questions were asked. Why are you so late? Is it fair that we all had to wait for you? Can't you be more aware of the time and be home when you're supposed to be?

Mom called Amanda in.

Dad asked Mom if she wanted wine and she did, and then he asked me if I wanted some. I looked at Mom, but she just kept staring at her hands. "Sure," I said, and he poured each of us a glass. Amanda got fruit juice that looked like wine.

"'All of life is a foreign country,'" our father said, raising his glass.

Mom frowned but drank her wine.

"Jack Kerouac," I said.

"Gandhi," Amanda said.

"Sounds like something Kerouac would say," Mom said. "Life. A foreign country. Sounds like him."

"What's that mean?" Dad said.

"You really want to know?"

It was mac and cheese night, which I appreciated. There was a complex salad with raisins and a lot of other stuff. There were sausages, too, for me. I was making a pile of mac and cheese on my plate and hoping Dad was smart enough to say no.

"Yes," he said.

"Wrong answer," I whispered.

He ignored me.

Mom said, "He never grew up. He never got over adolescent platitudes. Everything is a foreign country to him because he wants it to be that way. Never learn the ways of the world and become a part of it. That would be—what's the word?—'square,' in the vernacular of the times. He was forever a child."

I think Dad realized then I had been right. His face froze. Anger, but something else, too.

"I'd better get to work," he said, leaving almost all his food on his plate. He stopped at the doorway and looked back. He looked like he was about to ask a question, but he didn't. He turned and walked out of the house.

Mom stabbed a sausage with her fork. She held it up, and I thought for a moment she might actually eat it. She carefully put it back in the sausage dish.

"You two finish eating," she said. "I need to go calm down."

Amanda and I tried, but neither of us ate much. We didn't talk. I couldn't believe how quickly things could change. Just a few nights ago we'd all been fine. Now look at us. Broken.

"They love each other," Amanda said, echoing what I'd said earlier.

"Sure they do," I said.

Mom must not have been very successful in calming down, because she didn't come back to dinner. She didn't even come back down after dinner. Amanda and I watched TV. I called Gram to make sure she wasn't going to sneak off without me.

She said, "I'm waiting for something I need, and then we'll be ready."

"You promise you won't go without me?"

"Promise," she said.

"Mom and Dad are fighting," I said.

"I heard," Gram said, trying to sound neutral even though I knew she wasn't.

"They aren't even talking. I've never seen them like this."

"I'm sorry, Jack. I know it's hard on you and Amanda, but you just have to be patient and let them work this out."

"That's just it. I don't know what this is."

"That's for them to worry about," she said. "You just worry about you."

"Right."

"I mean it," she said. "You have to focus on your safety now. Let your mom and dad work out their own problems."

It became past Amanda's bedtime, and I had to tell her to go to bed, because Mom still hadn't come back downstairs.

"You have to take me."

So I carried her upstairs. She called Mom when I'd

got her tucked in. Mom came, but she didn't look good. Her face was puffy and red.

"We're going to be better," Amanda promised. "Me and Jack are going to be better."

Normally Mom would have been all over this. What did Amanda mean? Why would she say that? *This wasn't our fault.* But Mom just said, "You're good enough. Both of you are good enough."

Wow, thanks.

We left Amanda's room. Mom walked down the hall to her and Dad's bedroom.

"Are you all right?" I asked.

"Fine," she said, pausing in front of her door. "We're all going to be fine. Whatever happens. You know that, right?"

She didn't wait for an answer. She disappeared behind her door.

Before I could go back downstairs, Amanda called me into her room and asked me to read to her. She wanted me to read from *A Wrinkle in Time,* which Mom and Dad had read to her many, many times. I read. It took her a while to feel sleepy, which was unusual. Usually she was asleep after a few pages.

"Everything is going to be fine," she said. Her eyes were closed and her voice soft. She was halfway to sleep.

"Sure it will," I said, but I remembered Mom's "Whatever happens" and I wasn't sure at all.

I was heading back downstairs, debating which depressing movie to stream on Netflix, when my phone buzzed. It was Ash.

Ready whenever you are. Don't forget to bring the car.

I'd managed, in the family drama, to forget about our plan to visit Alice's dorm room and get her diary. Now I steeled myself for the theft. I just hoped it would go better than everything else was going in my life, but even at the time I had the feeling that hope wasn't going to be realized.

18

I got the keys out of Mom's purse and snuck out to her car. Fortunately our driveway had a steep incline, so I could put the car in neutral and coast out into the street before starting the engine. I just had to chance it from there. It wasn't the first time I'd "borrowed" Mom's car without asking. In my defense, I only did it when I knew she'd say no. Going out after nine on a school night was an automatic no.

I texted Ash back to let her know I was on my way.

She was waiting for me on the front steps of her parents' big blue house, dressed all in black, including black boots. Catwoman.

Meow.

"You look good," I said when she opened the passenger door and plopped onto the seat.

She ignored the compliment. "I better not get in trouble for this."

I frowned. "Would Bonnie say 'I better not get in trouble for this' to Clyde?" (See *Bonnie and Clyde,* 1967; writers: David Newman, Robert Benton; stars: Warren Beatty, Faye Dunaway.)

"Don't even start," she said. "You're no Clyde. I'm no Bonnie. I don't want to be arrested."

"Too late," I said.

I reminded her of our trip down to Iowa City, where we had the bad luck to be arrested for underage drinking (for one lousy beer!) because she was not fast enough during our escape. To be fair, she was in heels, but the party was mostly underage drinkers, which meant the cops had plenty of people to catch, so we should have got away. I led us out of the house and out the back door. All we had to do was clear a hedge and we were free. But Ash was grabbed by a female police officer who looked like she might have been a man once. I couldn't be sure — but she did have the body of the Rock and a hint of stubble. She made me think of the pro football player in *The World According to Garp* (1982; writers: John Irving, Steve Tesich; stars: Robin Williams, Mary Beth Hurt, Glenn Close), who became a woman and was a definite plus size.

"That policewoman was strong," Ash said defensively.

"You were slow."

"You try running in heels."

"No, thanks."

"Just don't get me arrested," she said.

"We aren't really even stealing," I said. "Alice told me to take her diary. Besides, you're just the lookout."

"What could possibly go wrong," she said, but I noticed it wasn't a question.

We parked the car in the library parking lot and walked across campus. Ash, in her tight black outfit, drew the eye of every male student we passed.

"You're attracting attention," I complained.

She said, "You want me to commit a felony *and* look bad?"

At least she wasn't wearing heels this time.

"It's not a felony."

"I looked it up," she said.

"Really?" I said.

"First-time offense for breaking and entering can be two to ten years."

"Jesus."

"Want to forget about it?" she said.

I did. I really did. But I thought about Alice's lost eyes. "We'll be fine. We won't get caught."

"Famous last words," she said.

I hoped those weren't my famous last words. I hoped for something more *Braveheart*-ish, like William Wallace's shout, "Freeeeeeeeeeedom!" (*Braveheart*, 1995; writer: Randall Wallace; stars: Mel Gibson, Sophie Marceau, Patrick McGoohan) or Spock's "I have been, and always shall be, your friend. Live long and prosper" (*The Wrath of Khan*, 1982; writers: Gene Roddenberry, Harve Bennett; stars: William Shatner, Leonard Nimoy, DeForest Kelley) or the really, really strong homicidal android in *Blade Runner* (1982; writers: Philip K. Dick, Hampton Fancher, David Webb Peoples; stars: Sean Young, Rutger Hauer, Harrison Ford), who said, "All those moments will be lost in time like tears in rain. Time to die." Now, those were some awesome famous last words.

Once again, the Nirvana dorm was unprotected. The college seemed to rely on charms, but whoever had made them didn't know what they were doing. The school would have been much better off with card swipes. We went into the dorm and up the stairwell.

"Just be ready to run," I advised.

"Why do I let you talk me into these things?" she said.

Why did she? For a girl so worried about her future and keeping her record pristine, she followed me into compromising situations pretty often.

We walked down the hall. The tape was there and the door closed. I tried the doorknob. It wouldn't turn.

She said, "Can we go home now?"

"Dead girl," I whispered, which was my way of summoning the dead. Sometimes it worked. Usually it didn't. "Dead girl. Dead girl."

Alice appeared, looking confused and groggy. She pushed her straight blond hair out of her eyes. "Did I fall asleep while we were talking?"

Then she looked around.

"This isn't the bathroom," she said.

"No sinks to flood," I said.

"Where is she?" Ash said.

"She's right in front of me," I said.

A slow and uncertain recognition came into Alice's face. "This is my dorm. My room. I haven't been able to come here since, since—"

"You died," I said.

The dead wanted to forget they were dead. It was best for everyone if they didn't.

"You wanted me to get your diary," I said.

"Did I?"

"You said you did."

"If she's changed her mind," Ash said, "let's get out of here."

"I need the diary," Alice said. "Now I remember. I need to know. I'll get it."

She tried to walk through the door but couldn't. There were places the dead could go and places they couldn't.

"Or you can get it for me," she said.

"I can't get into your room. It's locked and I don't have a key. Did you hide a spare?"

"We did," she said.

"Where?"

"Behind the—behind something. No, on top of it. I don't know." She was beginning to fade. Actually, she hadn't been all that solid to begin with.

Then she was gone.

"She said there's a key," I said.

"Where?" Ash said.

"Behind something. Or on top of it."

"Next time try to get clearer instructions from your dead person," Ash grumbled.

"She's not mine," I said.

"Whatever," she said.

But when I started looking around, feeling the top of the doorway frame and looking around for likely hiding places, she did, too. It took us a couple of minutes to exhaust all the places in the hallway.

"Wait a second," I said. My third eye saw the top of something that I recognized. I went back out into the stairwell, where I'd seen a fire hose in a case with a glass front. The top of it was about even with the top of my head. I reached up and felt around. Dirty. The cleaning people seemed to have missed this ledge entirely. I hated to think of how badly they would have done with dried creamed corn. And then I felt the key. I showed Ash.

"Great," Ash said, not sounding like she meant it.

"You can watch from out here," I offered.

She said she was an accessory anyway. She might as well do her part and try to keep us both out of jail.

I said, "If it's really a felony, we'd go to prison, I think."

"Shut up," she said.

We went back to the dorm door, and I put the key in and the lock snapped open. I crawled under the police tape that made an uneven X across the doorway.

I'd barely gotten over the threshold when I got a text. I looked at my phone and saw it was from Ash.

HURRY UP.

Is someone there?

JUST HURRY UP, BELL.

UR slowing me down.

Something about her all-caps orders to hurry up made me remember a time when she'd ordered me to slow down. We were eleven and in my tree house, which was awesome because I'd built it—with some pretty extensive help from my dad. Three stories. Anyway, Ash had decided she was going to teach me how to kiss, only I was so nervous about being caught that I kept trying to rush things.

"Slow down, Bell!" she'd said.

Some friends were coming over, including Blake, and if they saw me kissing her, I might as well transfer to another school. But she wanted to kiss, and I usually did what she wanted in those days. (These days, too, come to think of it.)

"You need to focus," Ash had said. So I tried to focus, and I think it must have worked because neither of us heard the arrival of my friends until it was too late.

"Eew, dude."

"No girls in the fort."

"This is our fighting place," Blake said. He sounded betrayed.

Of course, a couple years later I was considered a trailblazer for my early kissing with Ash. I suppose all the girls (not that there were *that* many) I kissed after Ash were judged against that first kiss. We were just kids, but . . .

I shook my head. It was stupid to even think about it.

I turned on the light by Alice's bed. I figured I'd start with the usual places: between the mattress and box spring, under the bed, behind the headboard, in her dresser drawers, in the recesses of her closet. Nothing. As I looked around, I began to feel kind of foolish. The police, trained and experienced, had searched this room. They had most likely found the diary.

What was I doing here?

Apparently, committing a felony.

Still, I kept looking. I heard a voice right outside the door. Male. I froze. My heart thumped like someone pounding on a door. Then the voice continued down the hall.

Felony, I thought. *I'm committing a felony.* Other people were applying to colleges and I was doing this.

Stupid. Stupid. Stupid.

I texted Ash: **U OK?**

She texted back: **JUST HURRY.**

I sat down on the bed. I'd looked everywhere. Even

though the diary likely wasn't even here, I still hated not finding it. I felt like I'd been sent on a wild-goose chase — and worse, I'd dragged Ash along. I guess that was why I got down on my hands and knees for one last look from a different perspective. At this point, what did I have to lose?

I crawled around and looked under the dresser, the desk, and finally under the bed again. I was about to turn away when I stopped. A piece of fabric hung from the box spring, so small that I'd missed it the first time I'd looked.

I slithered under the bed to where the tear was. It was too dark to see anything, so I reached my hand tentatively into the tear. Immediately I felt something small and leathery. I grabbed it and backed out from under the bed. I dusted off my clothes and opened the diary to the last entry, the one that Alice was so concerned about reading.

I feel so strange. I don't feel like me at all. Tonight I scratched B. when we were fooling around. I drew blood and I licked it. That's not me. I would never do that. He was totally freaked. "I don't even know you anymore," he said. And I said, "I don't know me, either." I feel like I'm going crazy.

My dreams, too, have been so strange the last few days. I've never had dreams like these. I know I —

That was as far as I got because the door swung open. The detective who'd chased me the day before stood in the doorway, holding Ash by the arm.

"I'll be," he said. "Found something, have you? Looks like you'll at least be going to prison for a reason."

"He snuck up behind me," Ash said apologetically.

"I'll take that," the detective said, holding out his hand.

He took the diary and took us down to the police station.

19

"Hello, Jack," the desk sergeant said.

I saluted him.

The detective said, "You two know each other?"

Later I would realize this was acting. He knew exactly who I was — and how many times I'd visited the station.

"Jack Bell," Sergeant O'Leary said. "He's a frequent flyer. Comes to visit us several times a year. Likes to sneak into the theater for a free movie now and then."

The detective held up the diary. "Now it's crossing police tape. Finding things we should have found."

"The boy has gifts."

"Don't," the detective said.

"I'm just saying. He has gifts. Could even be a finder."

I knew about finders. People whose gift — or curse, depending on your point of view — was finding things others deemed impossible to find. Sometimes a sock, sometimes a lost memory. Could be anything.

"If he is a finder," Ash said, "he's not a very good one. It took him forever to find that stupid diary."

"I'm not a finder," I said.

"See?" the detective said. "More of a loser, I'd say."

Sergeant O'Leary laughed. It sounded a little forced to me.

The detective motioned us down a narrow hall and to an interrogation room.

"Sorry," Ash whispered to me. "I got distracted by a text from Shelby. I didn't hear him until it was too late."

"I'm sorry I got you into this," I said.

The detective told us to have a seat at the table. The room was small and white, the metal table and chairs the only furniture in it. I was disappointed to see there was no one-way window.

"What in the Sam Hill were you two doing in that room?" the detective said.

I wondered if he'd ever interviewed suspects before. This was not the way it was done in the movies. He was supposed to try to act nice or dumb or something to get us to incriminate ourselves.

"We just thought we could help," I said.

"Help who?"

"Alice. We just thought, I thought, that I could help."

"So you knew the deceased?"

"Not exactly," I said, sneaking a look at Ash. I realized

that we'd made a novice's mistake in the world of crime. We didn't have a story worked out. I knew this detective wasn't going to believe I'd been taking instructions from the dead Alice.

Fortunately Ash was a quick thinker.

"I knew Alice," Ash said. "I'd met her, anyway. And her boyfriend, too. They seemed happy, in love. I told Jack I didn't think the boyfriend could've done it—killed Alice, I mean."

"So you break into a crime scene and disturb evidence because you'd met the victim and her boyfriend once and you two thought he wouldn't have killed her?" When he said it like that, I had to admit it sounded pretty lame.

"We didn't break in," I said. "There was a key."

"Where?"

I told him.

He turned to Ash. "The murder victim told you where the key was hidden?"

"No," Ash said. "She just mentioned something about a spare key when we were having coffee."

Ash was pretty good at this, I thought. Not good enough she should switch life goals, but pretty good.

"How'd you know about the diary?" the detective said.

"Alice told me about it," Ash said before I could come up with a lie. "She was joking about the things she wrote in her diary. I just thought maybe we could read it and see if it told us anything about what happened to her."

"And she told you where to find the diary?"

"No," Ash said, like this was a ridiculous question. "But we figured it was probably in her room somewhere. Jack volunteered to look for it."

"So how'd you find it, Jack?" the detective asked.

"It's kind of obvious, isn't it? I mean, people always hide things under the bed."

The detective's ruddy face became ruddier, and his narrowed eyes became narrower. Ash hid her smile with the back of her hand.

"You two wait here," he said. He made us empty our pockets and took our phones. Then he shut the door, locking us in.

Over an hour later, we were released into our parents' custody. My dad said he was disappointed. That was his usual line when I got in trouble. My mom told me she was even more disappointed than Dad. She recounted my bad behavior: I'd stolen her car, tampered with a crime scene, been arrested. Again. Did I want be locked up and no doubt become someone's sex slave (being a pretty boy) and only see family on weekends? Was that what I wanted?

Rhetorical question. I doubted even murderers *wanted* that. But my dad told me to answer my mom, so I said, "No, I do not want to be someone's sex slave." I knew being lectured by them shouldn't have made me happy, but it did—a little. They were working as a team. It was the first thing they'd done together in nearly a week.

"What on earth possessed you to break into a dead girl's dorm room?" Mom asked once we were home. I sat at the kitchen table while they paced around me.

I finally told them about the ghost, and that made Mom less angry. She knew that helping dead people could put you in bad positions sometimes.

"Still, Jack, you don't break the law, even to help them," she said. "That's one of Gram's rules."

"I know, but—"

"No buts."

"You know that boy confessed," Dad said.

"Alice said he didn't do it."

"So who does Alice say killed her?" Mom asked.

"That's the thing. She can't actually remember."

Mom frowned. "That is very troubling."

After another lecture about me stealing her car and breaking the law, Mom finally admitted that the police weren't going to charge me or Ash.

"I had a talk with the front desk sergeant, O'Leary. You were very lucky. The detective who caught you decided to let you off with a warning. Sergeant O'Leary said that diary was an important find, and the fact that you used a key to get in helped. But really you were just lucky the detective gave you a break."

Mom and Dad said they were going to discuss my punishment and let me know. This was a good sign. When they were really mad, judgment was passed immediately. Also, they were talking again. Another good sign.

When I got up to my room, I called Ash. I considered texting her, but I wanted to hear her voice. She picked up, and I apologized again for getting her into trouble.

"Forget it," she said.

"You're a really good liar," I said admiringly.

"Thanks," she said. "You're not so bad yourself."

"I just wish I'd had time to read more of the diary," I said. "At least getting arrested got my mom and dad talking again."

"Were they not talking?"

"Not much."

"Sorry," she said. "I know how it is."

She did. Her mom and dad separated a few years ago. They got back together after nine months, but she said it made her realize how you couldn't count on any relationship being permanent.

Everything could be broken.

"Just another reason you need to get out of this town," she said. "Get out on your own. Have your own life."

"I have my own life." Sometimes it seemed like I had too much life. But other times—she was right—not enough.

"I just mean," she said, "we need to move on."

She was very far away from me suddenly. Almost like she was already at college—like our lives together were already over and she had moved on. It was as if I'd stepped into the future and been smacked right in the face. She would be somewhere else and I would be here.

"Talk to you tomorrow," I said.

"You better," she said.

I tried to get to sleep, but I tossed and turned and tossed and turned. Everything was changing. And I wasn't ready. Ash was ready, though. She was looking forward to it. I wasn't sure I was looking forward at all. Why did everything have to change, even the things you didn't want to?

The queen makes her bargain with the king, accepting his terms. She will live in the king's prison with her lover. She will have a few slaves and some animals but nothing more.

The prison will be its own small universe. She will see the city only through the mists of time. She will not be able to leave the prison until she has completed the one act that will allow her to do so.

"And what is that?" she asks him.

"You must eat your mortal's heart," the king says. "It is the last part of the bargain. Eat it while he is alive and a door will open for you and you may return to the city. I may have found a new queen by then, but you will be allowed to return."

Though she hates him, she bristles at the thought that he will have a new queen. But she does her best not to let him see.

"We have a deal."

She loves Ishi, but perhaps the love will fade, and when it does, she will have a way back. Part of her believes it will never fade, that she will find a way for both of them to escape. And when she is free, she vows she will destroy the king.

In the meantime, the queen creates a palace in the prison, but she soon finds the king made the animals he gave her sterile. They die and there are none to replace them. In only a few years, the food supplies run low. The slaves are sterile, too. One by one they die away. She keeps a few alive with magic.

Her hatred for the king burns even hotter.

She keeps Ishi alive through magic, but she knows she cannot keep him alive for as long as she lives. He is short-liver. She keeps him young for over a hundred years. Death *comes for him every day, but she turns it away again and again. Two hundred years pass. He begins to age. And still she loves him, perhaps even more than when he was young.*

He begs her to eat his heart. "You will be trapped here all alone," he says.

She tries to imagine herself eating his heart, the door appearing, returning to the great city. Sometimes she does imagine it. But every time she does, she also imagines eating his heart, and this spoils everything. She cannot. She can. She cannot. She can.

20

The next morning I had two encounters before I even got to my first class. The first was far stranger than the second. There was a limousine parked out in front of the school, and as I rode by, the driver stepped out. He wore a dark suit and black cap that made him look totally gangster (in a movie sort of way).

"Jack Bell!" he shouted.

I pulled my bike around to the car.

"*Namaste.* Don't do drugs. Life is magic," the driver said. "Man in the car would like to speak with you."

I tried to look in the windows, but they were too dark to see in.

"His Holiness," the man said. "President of Nirvana College. Leader of spiritual people everywhere."

"Are you sure he wants to talk to me?"

"Jack Bell?"

"That's me."

"Man's waiting."

The Cowboy Guru himself, a Texan who wore bolo ties and cowboy boots, sat in the huge leather backseat, long legs stretched out, holding a cup of coffee in his hand. He had a goatee that made me think of the devil in *Heaven Can Wait* (1943; writers: Sam Raphaelson, Leslie Bush-Fekete; stars: Gene Tierney, Don Ameche, Charles Coburn) and wore a belt with a buckle the size of an iPhone.

"*Namaste*. Don't do drugs. Life is magic," he said with a Texas twang. "So nice to finally meet the famous Jack Bell."

"That would be my ancestor. I'm the unfamous Jack Bell."

"Modesty," he said. "Very becoming."

He didn't sound like he believed himself.

"I've seen your aura in dreams," he said.

That did not make me comfortable, but I knew the Cowboy Guru had a high respect for auras. There were entire courses devoted to their study at Nirvana College. I, on the other hand, not so much.

"It's good?" I said hopefully—in spite of myself.

"Bright as a searchlight, son. Red and green. Got a Christmas feel to it."

"I've always liked Christmas," I admitted.

"You like the presents, am I right? You like to open the little boxes and get the things you want."

"Who doesn't like presents?"

"Of course," he said, and winked. "I see a big Christmas for you this year. I see some very good things."

More discomfort. I wanted to get out of that car.

"Thanks," I said.

"Visualize with me," he said.

"Visualize?"

"Yourself, opening many, many wonderful presents. Do you see it?"

He closed his eyes. I kept mine open.

"Do you see it, Jack?"

"Sure," I said.

"Visualization is very important to us."

I didn't really want to think about Christmas. That meant thinking about family, and I was worried about mine just then.

"Thanks," I said, confused by the whole conversation and ready for it to be over.

"I see something else in your future."

There was something about his voice. Something hypnotic. It was almost like a gift. For just a second I believed there was a happy Christmas and something else in my future. His voice made me want to believe.

"You know, Jack, you're the kind of student we could use at Nirvana. Powerful aura. Good academically. Gifted. Just the kind of boy we'd like to give a scholarship to. A full scholarship with benefits."

I didn't know what to say. It cost a ton of money to go to Nirvana College.

I mumbled an ungracious thank-you.

"The police called and wanted to know if the college wanted to press charges against you and Sara White's daughter. I said no."

"I appreciate that," I said.

"You're welcome," he said. "Now I need you to do me a little favor. I need to know what you were after in that room."

There was no point in lying about it; the police had likely already told him what I'd found. "A diary. Her diary."

"How'd you know that it was there?"

"She told me," I said. I mean, he was His Holiness, president of Nirvana College, seer of auras and traveler of the astral planes (according to the Nirvana College brochure)—no reason to lie about talking to dead people.

"You knew Alice Highsmith?"

"Not knew. Know."

"Right," he said, winking. "Gotcha. But what was in the diary? Who else have you talked to? What do the police think?"

I realized something disturbing. He didn't believe I'd talked to Alice. That wink. That wink was all wrong. I got the feeling he didn't believe me because he didn't believe people could talk to the dead, which could not have been right, since he was who he was.

"She doesn't remember what happened to her."

"What happened to her was her boyfriend. Pushed her out the window. Very unfortunate," he said, shaking his head. "Very sad. Jealousy is a terrible thing. Did he mean to kill her? I doubt it. She's in a better place, you know. Told me herself."

He winked again. That wink was really beginning to piss me off.

"I'm going to be late for school," I said.

"Of course." But he leaned forward, holding me in place with his intense gaze. "Our mission is to enlighten the world," the Cowboy Guru said. "You understand how bad publicity could damage this great mission, don't you? You understand why it's important the police get that poor boy the help, the mental help, he needs."

"You're saying he had some kind of breakdown?" That could explain why he pushed Alice.

"We've hired lawyers to defend him. They assure me he will never see the inside of a prison. We just need to move on, Jack. The college needs to. You understand, right?"

"Yeah," I said. "I understand."

"Good. No more playing amateur detective. If the police contact you for any reason, you just give me a call."

Amateur? What was he talking about? I had the experience of dozens, maybe hundreds, of movie detectives behind me.

He handed me a card. "That's my private number. Normally you have to be a member of the hundred-thousand-dollar club to get it. Only for big donors. But it's for you, Jack. I think we're going to be good friends."

"Thanks," I said, because I felt like he expected me to say something.

"You say hello to Alice for me if you talk to her again," he said, and winked. "Now, you get your application for a scholarship in to the college as soon as you can. I have a very good feeling about your chances. *Namaste.* Don't do drugs. Life is magic." That wink really bothered me. A lot of things about "His Holiness" did.

The second encounter was with Sunday Parker, who was in front of the main entrance. She was a cheerleader with so much spirit she seemed to be cheering even when she was sitting in class. She blocked my way and asked me if I had school spirit.

I hesitated. Although I wouldn't have said that I had school spirit, I had met many spirits. I didn't think Sunday Parker would want to hear about those spirits, though.

"Some days I do and some days I don't." My answer disappointed both of us.

"We're selling raffle tickets to support the football team," she said. "It's important that everyone partici-pates."

Sunday was very pretty, with her blond ponytail and perky little body, but for some reason I had never felt the least bit attracted to her. I was definitely in the minority.

"Why?" I asked.

"We all need to be a part of the team," she said, a little put out that I would even need to ask.

I bought two tickets. Sunday Parker was a little disappointed by this, too.

"Can we count on you for the rally before the game tonight?"

"Of course," I lied.

She smiled. It was one of those full-court-press smiles. Her cheer came back into her face. I'd known Sunday Parker all my life—*known* might be too strong a word; I'd been in classes with her, seen her at school—and she'd always been like this.

"Good," she said. "They're crowning me, you know."

"No," I said. "Crowning you what?"

"I was the runner-up in the pageant. Corn Queen. Now that the winner is, you know, dead, they want me to take over."

"Are you sure you want to be crowned?" I said.

"I know. It's totally too soon. The pageant officials are freaked, though. They have some fund-raiser next week. Anyway, you can see me crowned. That will be nice."

"Okay," I said, though I wasn't sure why it would be nice, exactly. Or even who she meant it would be nice for. Officially, she had been the second most beautiful girl in the county and now she was the most beautiful girl, so I guess that might have been nice for her.

SCREENPLAY IDEA: Girl who is officially the second most beautiful girl in the county murders the most beautiful girl in the county in order to become Corn Queen. But once she does, the ghost of the murdered girl starts to haunt her. (Or so we think.) She's driven mad. She is stripped of her title when she comes to school naked and confesses her crime. But it turns out the murdered girl wasn't haunting her at all. It is the girl who will now be the new Corn Queen who suspected the ex–Corn Queen had murdered her predecessor. She skillfully drove her mad. The last image is of the new Corn Queen smiling as the ex–Corn Queen is taken away by the police. Horror film with some comic elements. *(Major summer release.)*

I went to the bathroom a few times that day and I didn't see Alice once, which was both a relief and a disappointment. But maybe since I found the diary, she'd remembered what had happened somehow and had been able to go on to wherever the dead go on to.

I didn't seek out Ash at the smoking wall over lunch. Instead, I sat in the cafeteria and ate lunch with Chris, Blake, and the twins. I told them about meeting the Cowboy Guru, which they thought was totally weird.

"What did he want?" Blake asked. "Talk over old *X-Files* episodes?"

I had seen them all. Blake thought they were stupid.

"He wanted to talk about giving me a scholarship," I said, leaving out important parts of our conversation.

"'*Namaste*. Don't do drugs. Life is magic,' my ass," one of the twins said.

"He's deeply misguided," the other said.

"Do you think he means pot, too, when he says no drugs?"

They argued this point and it was a pretty stupid argument.

After lunch, Chris hung back with me and said that I'd better be careful.

"Mom says His Holiness is dangerous."

"Dangerous how?"

"She said people who don't believe in anything are always dangerous."

"That sounds right."

"Mom's usually right about people."

"More lucky guesses?" I said.

"How'd you guess?"

We planned another poker game for later in the week. He said I could talk to his mother while I was over. I knew he was trying to help, but I didn't think talking to Mrs. Harris was going to improve my situation. I was going to have to deal with the Cowboy Guru myself. Maybe I could deal with him in a way that would let me get that scholarship. I could get a college degree right here in Utopia.

That wouldn't be such a bad thing. That might be a really good thing.

I served another hour of my detention that afternoon with a jock named Bobby and a goth girl named Cassandra. It was not all Breakfast Club (See *The Breakfast Club*, 1985; writer: John Hughes; stars: Emilio Estevez, Judd Nelson, Molly Ringwald). We didn't talk that much, but Cassandra—who was reading a book called *Poems from the Dark Side*—did say my "Creamed corn or death!" shout in first-day assembly was pretty awesome.

"Yeah," Bobby agreed. "Totally."

So there was that momentary convergence of social groups over the short-lived but potent creamed-corn revolt, but that was it.

Mrs. Archer let us out ten minutes early because she had a hair appointment, which normally would have improved my mood but didn't for some reason.

I decided to risk sneaking into the movies. I climbed the first building, made the jump between the two, and climbed down the ladder. I was aware that I might watch the same movie as the day before, but there was always the chance it would be a new one. Mr. Goodfellow was unpredictable that way.

I was lucky. *Casablanca* was playing (1942; writers: Julius and Philip Epstein; stars: Humphrey Bogart, Ingrid Bergman). I got to the point where Ilsa tells Rick that she can't fight it anymore—she loves him and has to be with him, even if it means damaging Victor Laszlo and his fight against the Nazis. This is big stuff. She's saying that her love for Rick is more important than anything, even the world war. Talk about love conquering all.

What did my mom and dad's love have to conquer? Money problems, maybe the problems of people whose dreams hadn't exactly come true. It made me kind of sad to think that about the dreams, but at the same time it wasn't like they had to, you know, overcome a world war or anything.

As I was thinking this, maybe obsessing over it, I heard someone behind me. It turned out to be Mr. Jenkins trying to sneak up on me and doing a worse job than Amanda ever did. I made a run for it. He tried that ever-impressive and totally ineffectual "Stop!" I banged out the door and into the alley.

I ran, but it wasn't necessary. He didn't come after me. Usually he did, though my grandmother could run faster than he could. Still, I hoped he was feeling all right. Escaping his lame attempts to capture me was part of the fun of sneaking into the movies.

On my way home, I thought about the end of the movie. Humphrey and Ingrid don't get together. Love isn't enough after all. The plane flies off into the night, and Ingrid and her noble husband are on it and Humphrey and the little French officer are walking off into the night. It's a great ending—the best worst ending ever — but it scared me because I'd never doubted that my mom and dad were in love and so never really believed they'd get divorced. But what if love wasn't always enough? Look at Ingrid and Humphrey.

For the first time, I believed it was possible Mom and Dad might not make it after all.

Every morning the queen wakes planning to kill her lover. She has killed many to become queen, many of her own kind. Many short-livers. She knows how to kill. Ishi is dying. It is time to send him on his way. She can do no more.

Every morning she comes up with many reasons to kill Ishi, but every night she resolves to live with him in this prison for as long as he lives. Better to be in this prison with Ishi than in the greatest city the world has ever known without him.

This thought makes her feel noble sometimes and pathetic others.

Love, she thinks, is a prison. Love holds her. That is what keeps her in this place. It is not the king. It is not his awesome power or his hatred — it is love.

She listens for her lover's heartbeat and hears it. As powerful as she is, she sometimes thinks she will go mad. Love is madness.

21

We ate another silent family dinner that night. Even Amanda hardly talked. Finally, desperate to break the silence, I started talking about Ash's and my arrest and reminded them that they hadn't given me my punishment yet. I thought maybe a week without phone and TV was fair. Mom said that they'd decided not to punish me at all. Instead of feeling relieved, I felt mad.

What was wrong with them?

SCREENPLAY IDEA: A boy wakes up one morning, and his parents look the same, but they aren't. He slowly discovers that they've been replaced by androids. He realizes that this is happening everywhere. Who or what is slowly replacing all the parents with androids? Why? To what end? *(Horror. Indie film, limited release.)*

"I need to be punished for my actions," I said, turning my focus back to my parents' irresponsible parenting.

"Not this time," Mom said.

She went back to moving her food around on her plate. My dad just stared off into space. What was wrong with these people? I reminded her that I'd stolen her car (normally I would have said "borrowed") in addition to getting arrested.

"The dead girl is a mitigating circumstance," Mom said.

"You're getting off this time, buddy," Dad said. "Let's just talk about something else."

We didn't actually talk about anything else. It seemed like we didn't have anything else to talk about.

I decided to ground myself. I didn't go to the pep rally or the football game with Blake and the twins. I stayed in my room and read a novel. I would parent myself if they weren't up to the job. I thought more about my screenplay. I decided that the android parents were all part of a plan by a giant company to brainwash the next generation into helping them conquer the world. The android parents didn't care one bit for their children. Not one bit.

For the second night in a row I had to put Amanda to bed. We read a little more of A Wrinkle in Time.

"Do you think Gram can make a love potion?" Amanda asked.

"Possibly," I said. "You have a boy in mind?"

"No."

I crouched down by the bed and brushed back a strand of her long hair that had fallen over her face. "They don't need a love potion," I said. "They love each other."

"You could ask her," Amanda said. "Just in case."

I started to say, again, that they didn't need it, but then I said, "I'll ask her."

"Can you sit there while I fall asleep?"

She hadn't needed anyone to sit with her for a long time.

"Sure," I said.

After Amanda fell asleep, I went out onto the porch to get out of the house for a while. Captain Pike was sitting on his porch smoking his pipe. I crossed the lawn, which shimmered from moonlight. The moon floated over us in the night sky, full and bright.

Lucy, Captain Pike's bird, was making a lot of noise. She was talking about the moon, "the beautiful moon," as she did sometimes when it was full. Then she did something I'd never heard her do. She recited poetry.

"Strange fits of passion have I known:
And I will dare to tell,
But in the Lover's ear alone,
What once to me befell.

When she I loved looked every day
Fresh as a rose in June,
I to her cottage bent my way,
Beneath an evening-moon.

Upon the moon I fixed my eye,
All over the wide lea;
With quickening pace my horse drew nigh
Those paths so dear to me.

And now we reached the orchard-plot;
And, as we climbed the hill,
The sinking moon to Lucy's cot
Came near, and nearer still.

In one of those sweet dreams I slept,
Kind Nature's gentlest boon!
And all the while my eye I kept
On the descending moon.

My horse moved on; hoof after hoof
He raised, and never stopped:
When down behind the cottage roof,
At once, the bright moon dropped.

What fond and wayward thoughts will slide
Into a Lover's head!

'O mercy!' to myself I cried,
'If Lucy should be dead!'"

"She's never done that before," Captain Pike said.

"What was that?"

"William Wordsworth." Captain Pike pulled his pipe out of his pocket. "Wordsworth. She's been holding out on me. All these years she could have been reciting poetry."

I was about to ask him if he'd read the poem to her recently or something when the screen door creaked open. We both turned to look. The parrot had somehow gotten out of her cage and pushed open the door. She flew right past us. We both grabbed for her and we both missed.

"Lucy!" Captain Pike shouted.

He leaped out of his chair. He was over a hundred years old, but he made a pretty good jump. We both ran into the front yard, but the parrot was too fast for us. She flew up into the night, heading straight for the moon. For a moment she was a shadow against the pale white disk, and then she was swallowed in the darkness.

"I've lost her," Captain Pike said softly, staring at where she'd been. Then he looked at me. "Had her for forty years, you know. Stupid bird always wanted to fly to the moon. Crazy thing for a bird to want."

"I didn't realize she was that old," I said.

"She was locked in her cage. I always keep her in her cage when the moon is full."

"I guess she figured a way out."

"Aye," he said. "But how?"

Rhetorical question. He saw many things with that glass eye of his. Much more than I could. If he didn't know, I sure didn't.

"I'm sorry," I said.

"Not your fault," he said. "Is it?"

"Not this time," I said, though sometimes it seemed like everything was my fault. "Could she—?" I stopped myself.

"Could she what?"

"Maybe make it to the moon?"

He shook his head and headed back up onto the porch, and I followed. We sat back down and he got his pipe lit again.

"Something is wrong, Jack. Murder. My glass eye has been hurting me for days. Now this. This town—there's something wrong. Stirrings of some kind."

Suddenly I felt what I thought might be a stirring. Then I realized it was just my phone vibrating. I didn't answer and it didn't buzz, so whoever it was didn't leave a message.

"What kind of stirrings?" I said.

"Something is keeping me from seeing, Jack. And now poor Lucy is off to the moon. I feel something I've never felt before. I feel threatened here in Utopia."

My phone vibrated again—this time a text. "Sorry," I said to Captain Pike, taking my phone out of my pocket and looking at the screen. It was from Sunday Parker, who was in my contacts list because we'd been in a study group together last year. Even then, though, she'd never texted me. Now the text read: I need to see you now. It's life or death. Meet me at Utopia Park.

This was a bizarre text on many levels. First, why me? Second, "life or death"? Sunday may have been way too enthusiastic when it came to school spirit, but she wasn't really a drama queen about anything else. Life or death?

"You'd better go," Captain Pike said. "She needs you."

I didn't ask how he knew what the text said. I knew. Glass eye.

"Can you see her?" I said.

"Not now," he said. "For just a second—then she was gone."

I was reluctant to leave him. He'd just lost Lucy, after all, his companion for forty years. I knew he was hurting. Still, there was that whole "life or death" part to the message. I got on my bike and rode off to the park. That was my first mistake.

22

My second mistake was not turning my bike around as soon as I saw her standing in the park under a big birch tree. It was a full moon, and sometimes people looked unworldly in the milky white and heavy shadows of a full moon. But I knew it wasn't just a trick of the moonlight that made Sunday Parker appear ghostly; it was because she was ghostly.

I pulled up next to her. "Sunday Parker," I said, trying to think of how I might tell her she was dead.

"Do I look totally disgusting?" she said. "I feel so pale. I must look a mess. I can't remember why, but I must."

"You look fine," I said, and didn't add—for a dead person.

"I guess the rumors are true. About you, I mean. Gifted or whatever. I suppose there are others like you?"

"Some, but most who have different gifts—or curses, depending on your point of view."

"My father and mother were always so adamant no one in Utopia had special powers. Utopia is just a good Midwestern town. A simple place. They always said that."

"It is those things, too," I said. "Just some people here have unique talents. That's all."

"I suppose I knew deep down. Funny how you can fool yourself."

"I'm sorry you're dead."

"You didn't come to the rally, did you?" she said, sounding hurt.

"No," I admitted, and wished I had or had at least bought more tickets from her. "I've been going through some things," I added lamely.

"Tell me about it," she said.

"Right. Sorry. What happened to you, anyway?"

"Something strange," she said slowly.

"How did you die?"

Her face looked blank. "I'm not sure. I knew a moment ago—didn't I?"

"You don't remember how you died?" What was with all these dead girls not remembering the details of their deaths? I tried to think of ways she might have died that didn't involve someone else purposely causing it. "Maybe you were run over or you had some kind of seizure or something?"

"Do I look like I was run over to you?" she said,

sounding more horrified by the thought she might look bad than the fact that she was dead. I wondered if she'd accepted the one-way nature of death. No coming back. No need to worry about being messed up.

"The dead don't bleed," I said, trying to reassure her. "They look like they did in life, except very pale and thin."

"I was thin," she snapped.

"You were," I agreed. "What's the last thing you remember?"

"I cheered at the game. I remember that."

"And after that?"

"Um, as I was leaving the stadium, Moose hit on me. Then I — then I — I'm not sure. I called you?"

"Moose hit on you?" I said. That didn't sound like Moose. He was a big linebacker who wasn't, as my father would say, the sharpest tool in the shed, but he was a nice guy off the football field. He liked my movie reviews for the school paper and told me he wished he could write like I did. Moose was strange in that way. He was a star on our very bad football team, but he was always wishing he could do what someone else could do. He was probably the one player on the team who could get a football scholarship to a college, but he didn't want to.

"He asked me to go eat pizza with him," Sunday Parker explained.

"I wouldn't exactly call that hitting on you."

"Puh-lease," she said.

"Not good enough for Sunday Parker?" I said, forgetting for a moment that she was dead.

"I didn't mean it like that."

"Of course not," I said.

"I was never mean to him or any boy who asked me out. Boys have it so easy. They don't get asked out all the time by girls they aren't interested in."

I hadn't really thought of it that way, but it was true, I guess.

"Where was he when he asked you out?" I said.

"In the parking lot. So I was in the parking lot."

"But you didn't get in his car?"

"I told him I had to go home, but that was a lie."

"Where'd you go?"

She hesitated. "I was going over to Eric Flute's house."

Last I'd heard, Eric Flute was dating Sunday Parker's best friend, Emily Fairfield.

"Emily's boyfriend? That Eric Flute?"

"Yes, that Eric Flute. I was just going to stop by for a minute, though."

"To see Emily?"

"Emily wasn't there. But—I—it's really none of your business."

"Fine," I said. "I'm out of here."

"Wait."

"If you want my help moving on, you need to tell me the truth."

She hesitated. "I was hooking up with Eric."

"You drove over to his house?"

"I got in somebody's car to go to Eric's, but then I'm not sure what happened. I remember thinking that I needed something." She shook her head. "I can't remember what I needed. And I can't remember what happened. It's like I wasn't there but I was."

"Were you in Eric's car?" I said.

"No, he wouldn't have driven me. We were careful." Her eyes wouldn't meet mine. "We never drove anywhere together. I always parked a few blocks away from his house, and he did the same when he came to mine."

"Maybe you were in your car with someone. Were you driving?"

"Maybe," she said. "I called you. Why would I call you?"

"I'm different. Maybe you knew you were dying?"

"Maybe. You should have answered your phone."

"No offense, but we were never really friends."

"Do something for me anyway? Make a call."

"To who?"

"Someone. The authorities. The police. My body is right over there, all—you know—alone."

I hadn't noticed, but now I did. Her body lay just a few feet away. It looked empty in a way her ghost didn't.

"They'll find you," I said, looking away from the body.

"Please," she said. "I don't want someone else to see me that way."

She began to fade. I'd seen this many times before. It was as if she could only last so long in the world now that she wasn't really in this world anymore.

"Please," she said. "Please, Jack. Promise. Please."

"OK," I said reluctantly.

Another stupid promise to a dead girl.

Then I was all alone with the body of Sunday Parker. I considered riding away, but in the end I did what I'd promised. I called the police. That was my third mistake.

One day Ishi dies. Death comes, and all the queen's spells fail to make it leave. She tries then to wrestle Death into submission, but Death is too strong even for her. It takes Ishi and promises to return for her one day.

The queen pulls Ishi's heart out of him immediately. She eats it. The door of the prison does not open. Was she too late or did the king lie?

The queen's anger raises a storm in her prison; her emotions fill the skies. The animals and slaves (she has finally found a way to overcome the king's sterility spell and slowly she is rebuilding her herds) all cower as the storm cracks with lightning and rain pelts the earth like bullets shot from above. Her heart rages.

Ishi is gone and she is trapped.

Alone.

How could she be so stupid?

Years pass.

Years and years.

One day she knows the city has disappeared. It was a city of magic, and when it goes, it is as if it has never been. This is another thing to mourn. Her only solace is that the king must be dead. He would never let the city die if he was alive. Then she knows they are all dead. Gods — well, close to gods. And still it is as if none of them ever were. She is the last of her kind.

She spends her days looking for a way out. Hundreds of years become a thousand. There is no way. She finally admits this. Ishi's beating heart was her only way. The heart that no longer beats.

But then she has a thought.

Maybe there is another way.

23

My fourth mistake was not riding away after I called the police. I waited because I didn't want the body to be alone. The first police car drove into the park with its spotlight on. I waved when it flashed over me.

The police car pulled up beside me and shined the light right in my face. Two officers got out. One of them asked me if I was armed.

"No," I said, "of course not."

"Step forward, please. Hands on head."

"I just found her," I said. "I called you."

"Put your hands on your head and step forward. Now."

So I did, and when I did, one of the officers hurried over to Sunday's body. The other one frisked me to make sure I wasn't carrying a weapon. He told me he was removing my wallet so he could get my ID. I didn't say anything.

"Her neck's broken," the cop over by Sunday said. "Bruises. Beaten up pretty bad. Better call Bloodsmith."

"Don't move," the cop who had my ID said, and took a few steps back and called someone.

"You know who the victim is?" the other cop asked.

"Sunday Parker," I said. "She's in my class at school."

"High school?" he said.

"Yeah."

"Pretty girl."

I don't know why I said it. "She was Corn Queen."

"Was she? Is she your girlfriend?"

"No."

"You just happened along."

"I was out riding."

Another cop car pulled up. Another cop got out, an older one, who I recognized.

"Jack Bell," he said. "What are you doing here?"

Two summers ago he arrested a bunch of us for swimming in the Utopia Park swimming pool around midnight. It was a warm night and we were just cooling off, but there was the matter of a fence and a CLOSED sign. It was a failing in me that a closed sign and a locked gate made swimming in the pool more fun.

"I found the body," I said.

"You'd better wait for the detective, then," the cop said.

"My mom will worry."

"Call her," he said.

I called her.

Detective Bloodsmith arrived about fifteen minutes later. When he saw me, he said, "You just keep showing up where you shouldn't."

He had a point.

"This time I was just—unlucky."

Kind of the truth.

"Unlucky," he said, making it sound more like "unlikely."

He went over to the body. "Doesn't look too good."

The cop who knew me said, "She's the unlucky one."

"Check the boy's hands?"

"No, sir."

Bloodsmith told him to do it now. The cop checked my hands. He told me to tell the truth and I'd be OK.

Then the detective got Sunday Parker's cell phone out of her pocket and pressed what turned out to be the last number she'd dialed. My phone rang.

"What do you know about that?" Detective Bloodsmith said.

That was enough for them to decide that I needed to go down to the station for more questioning. They read me my rights and then cuffed me—which they'd never done before and which made me realize just how much more serious this was than the other things I'd done— and I was driven to the station.

Detective Bloodsmith wanted a narrative of my night. He wanted to know all about Sunday Parker and me.

"Of course if you don't want to talk to me, that's your right. Makes you look guilty, but you have your rights."

"I don't want to talk to you," I said, "but I will."

"How do you think Ms. Parker died, Jack?"

"The officer said her neck was broken."

"Come on, Jack. A little rough sex that got out of hand?"

"No!" I said. "We didn't have sex."

"What did you have?"

"Nothing."

"Come on, Jack. She called you right before she died. You must have had something. Why you?"

I couldn't tell him without telling him the truth, which I couldn't tell him. He wouldn't believe me.

"Are you covering for someone?"

"I was out on a bike ride."

"Next you'll be making up stories about dead people calling you or bad magic or some nonsense."

"Dead people can't use the phone."

"What really happened, Jack?"

"I rode past the park. I should have turned the other way."

"Two dead girls. One Jack Bell. Let's go back to Alice for a minute."

SCREENPLAY IDEA: A homicidal homicide detective has it in for a boy in town. In fact, he hates him so much that he kills two girls just so he can arrest him for the murders. It turns out that the boy is the detective's son and the boy's mother died in childbirth. He blames the boy for killing his wife. He gave him up for adoption so he wouldn't harm him, but then through a coincidence (to be determined) he stumbles on his identity. He has to make him pay. Dark. *(Film festival circuit. Should be big on the small screen: TV, DVD.)*

The detective kept the interrogation going for a while. Finally he sighed and sat back and put his hands behind his head.

"This isn't going to end well for you, Jack," he said. "I'd like to help you out if I can, but I can't if you keep lying to me."

I knew he wouldn't like the truth any better. Dead girl asked me to call the police so her body wouldn't be there all alone. He wasn't going to go for that. So the only way to convince him I wasn't lying was to lie.

"Bike ride," I said.

He finally told me to get the hell out.

"But don't leave town," he said.

I said, "I thought that was just TV. I didn't think cops really said that."

"We'll surprise you," he said.

Mom and Dad were waiting for me out in the police station lobby. They were not happy.

"What have you done now?" Dad said.

"All they would tell us was that they needed you to answer questions before they could let you go. They said we might want to hire a lawyer."

"Let's just get out of here," I said, tired and angry.

They agreed, reluctantly, but demanded the whole story the moment we were in the truck. When I'd told them everything, Dad said, "You say the detective is a nonbeliever?"

"Totally. Worse than my friend Blake. He's got denial written all over him. Bold print. I'm talking—"

"We get the idea," Mom said.

"What's the detective's name?" Dad asked.

"Detective Bloodsmith. He's pretty intense."

"Bloodsmith?" my father said. "Are you sure?"

"Kind of a distinctive name," I said.

"Did you know he was back?" Dad said, looking at Mom.

"Back?" I said.

"Someone may have mentioned that he moved back," Mom said. "I wasn't really paying attention."

"You guys know him?" I said.

"He was your mom's boyfriend before she and I got married," Dad said.

"Her boyfriend?" I said.

"Didn't end well," Dad said.

"He'll be fair," Mom said.

"Don't count on it," Dad growled.

"He was always fair," she said.

"Wait," I said. "Go back a little. Mom's boyfriend? I thought you guys got together in high school. You always said that. You were dating as sophomores."

"We were," they both said.

If nothing else, my situation had gotten them answering in unison again, which made me feel better for a second or two.

"But your father disappeared," Mom said. "He went off on his whatever, his trip. Got lost. Forgot about me. I thought he was gone for good."

"I was on a quest," Dad said. "I was never lost. I was searching. And I never forgot about you."

Sometimes he compared himself—though, wisely, not this time—to the hit man, Jules, in *Pulp Fiction* (1994; writers: Quentin Tarantino, Roger Avary; stars: John Travolta, Uma Thurman, Samuel L. Jackson), who has a revelation in a diner that he needs to wander America like Kwai Chang Caine (*Kung Fu*; TV show, 1972–75; star: David Carradine). My father would say he had that same revelation and left Utopia, but he always knew he would come back to my mother.

"All I know is your father left. He said he had to go find himself. I said look in a mirror, but you know your father, has to do things his own way."

"So you broke up?" I asked.

"We decided we would see other people," she said. "It was your father's idea."

This was a shocking revelation.

"We were young," Dad said. "All we knew was each other. We agreed it would be good, during our separation, to see others. Make sure we were right for each other. I just didn't think your mother would embrace it so completely."

"So while you were off screwing girls, you expected me to remain chaste?" Mom said.

I groaned. My parents had missed the parenting-book section on discretion around your offspring.

"No. But I didn't expect you to get a boyfriend. I didn't expect you to get serious with anyone."

"Well, I did."

"And now look what's happened. He's out to get our son."

"I doubt that," she said. "Our son is perfectly capable of getting himself into trouble."

"A dying girl sent me a text," I reminded her.

"Yes," she said. "Another very strange and terrible event. But why do they keep involving you?"

"That's what the detective asked," I said, feeling she was siding with him. Then I added, "Anyway, how could you be with someone like Bloodsmith who doesn't even believe in ghosts?"

She shrugged. "It was one of the things that came between us even before your father came between us.

He was — probably still is — convinced that the town had created a kind of psychosis with all its superstitions. He planned on changing things."

"Didn't get very far with that," Dad said triumphantly.

"He ran for city council. He thought he'd start there, really try to rid the town of what he thought were its superstitions. He got carried away and made it sound like a witch hunt. I'm afraid a lot of people were angry with him about his attitude. He got a very bad rash — I still don't know who hexed him — but he and I broke up about that time. He left not long after that. I'm surprised to see him return."

"I think he might still be angry," I said.

"I wouldn't be surprised," Dad said. "'A quick temper will make a fool of you soon enough.'"

I thought about this. "Bruce Lee?"

Dad waited for Mom to make a guess, but she didn't. "Excellent," my father said to me.

And then a silence fell over us, and Dad turned on the radio to his classic-rock station to fill it. An old Aerosmith song was playing, "Dream On." Normally Dad would sing along. He was a terrible singer, but for some reason I enjoyed listening to him. Something stopped him then, though. I guess none of us felt like singing that night.

24

That weekend I stayed home. I hardly went out of the house. I talked on the phone, texted, e-mailed, surfed the Net, and watched all the Harry Potter movies. Maybe I was hiding out a little, but it felt good to be alone and just think. No dead girls. No live ones, either.

Monday morning, first thing, vice principal Sanderson reported the death of Sunday Parker on the announcements. He advised us that the police were looking into the possibility that her death was no accident and we should all be cautious in our activities. Girls cried. A boy or two looked close to crying. When I came out of my first class, the hallway was knotted with people all talking at once.

People weren't murdered in Utopia—bad things happened from time to time just like anywhere else, but not murder. A Nirvana student's possible murder was bad enough, but someone from town, a local—that was shocking. People were afraid. It was in their faces. I felt it in mine.

What I noticed over the day was that people's eyes began to rest a little too long on me. A few gave in to rude staring. Somehow it had gotten out that I had found the body. Then Blake told me that he and some of my other friends had been called into the principal's office to talk to Detective Bloodsmith.

"What the hell, dude? What happened?"

"I found her," I said.

"Yeah, right, just out riding your bike?"

"She called me."

"That detective was acting like he thought you were doing her. Were you?"

"No."

"I always wanted to. Now I guess I'll never get the chance."

He was just being Blake, but Sunday Parker was dead and that was his reaction? He wouldn't get to do her?

"You can be a real dick," I said, and walked away.

"At least I'm not a murder suspect!" he yelled after me.

That got me a lot more looks as I walked down the hall. I walked quickly.

Ash caught up with me after lunch and said we should skip afternoon classes and go have coffee some-where. I was all for it—tired of suspicious stares and irritating questions. We went to the only coffeehouse in town besides my dad's, Bad Brew.

Ash said she'd been interviewed by Detective Bloodsmith, too.

"He kept implying you and Sunday Parker—"

"We weren't."

"He doesn't like you much."

"The feeling is mutual," I said.

"This isn't some guy thing, is it?" she said.

"What do you mean?"

"You know what I mean. A guy thing. You're not provoking him, are you?"

"No," I said. "He's just a jerk."

"I'm worried you're engaging in self-destructive behavior," she said. "Provoking him won't prove anything."

This sounded like classic Nathaniel psychobabble.

"I didn't know you were taking a psychology class."

"All right," she said. "But you do start fights sometimes that you know you can't win. You're not going to win a fight with this detective. Antagonizing him isn't the right move."

I wondered if this was true and if she was another fight I couldn't win. Thankfully, before I had more thoughts along this pathetic line, I got a call. Gram.

"Jack? It's your grandmother," she said. Never mind that I'd told her about a hundred times that cell phones had caller ID. "I'm going to the spirit world tomorrow night. If you can manage to stay out of jail long enough to come over, I'd appreciate your presence."

"I'll be there," I said.

I saw my grandmother (my third eye) sitting barefoot on her porch (she seldom wears shoes), smoking a cigar.

"You're smoking," I said.

"Mind your own business," she said.

She was supposed to give up cigars. My mother had insisted when Gram got bronchitis last year.

"I won't tell Mom this time, but you owe me."

"You sound like your little sister. She found my stash of cigars and said the same thing. Did you teach her that?"

"She taught me," I said.

"Keep your third eye open and use it to better purposes than spying on me."

"I'll see you tonight," I said.

"You really weren't sleeping with Sunday Parker?" Ash said when I'd hung up.

"Not me."

"Someone said you were. I don't like to be lied to."

"Who said that?"

"You know Whitney?"

There was only one Whitney at our school. Whitney Adams. Tall. Blond. Overly perky.

"I don't *know* know her," I said. "But I know who she is."

"She thinks Sunday Parker was seeing you in secret. To quote her, you two were 'doing it.'"

"Doing what?" I said in an attempt to make Ash squirm, but she just arched an eyebrow.

"So Whitney is wrong?" she said.

"Why would we see each other in secret?"

"I don't know. Maybe her parents hate juvenile delinquents. Some parents are unreasonable that way."

I shrugged. "Sunday Parker isn't my type. Wasn't."

"Whitney seemed pretty convinced that Sunday Parker was seeing someone. If not you, then who?"

I couldn't tell. I wanted to. Gram said that when a dead person told you something, it had to be in confidence. We had our gifts—or curses, depending on your point of view—for a reason, and when dead people spoke to us, it was like they were talking to their doctor or something. Privileged information.

"She wasn't seeing me," I said

"Good," Ash said.

"Why good?"

"Motive."

Once I got over my disappointment that Ash wasn't jealous, a thought struck me: Eric Flute had a motive to kill Sunday Parker. A secret boyfriend whose girlfriend was best friends with the victim—motive.

"You should be more careful now," Ash said.

"About what?"

"About everything. You are not a careful person."

"I talk to dead people," I said.

"You go out of your way to be stupidly careless. Like sneaking into the theater. Maybe you should be a little more careful for a while."

"I talk to dead people," I said again.

"So?"

"So sometimes I need to do something not careful to feel alive."

"It's a small town. You've been in the gossip news too much lately."

"Let them talk."

"Not a good attitude. There are people in this town who would love to see you in real trouble. And not just because they don't like troublemakers. You know what I mean."

I guess there were people like that. I didn't think about them much, but besides the Utopians in denial, there were some who believed in the gifted (or cursed) but thought of us as freaks. Some of them would have loved to have a Utopia without us. Ash was probably right. I should be more careful.

"I'm so tired of this small town," she said. "Aren't you?"

"Sometimes," I said. "Sometimes I can't see myself anywhere else."

"I'll be glad to start new. I want to go someplace where no one thinks they know me."

"That would be cool."

"You don't sound like you mean it," she said, "but you should. They think they know you here."

"Sometimes it seems like nobody knows anybody."

"Now *you* sound like Nathaniel," she said.

"No need to get insulting," I said.

She gave me a look but didn't say anything.

We finished our lattes. It was too late to go back to school for my last class, so I saw no reason to go back for detention. I rode my bike home by way of the sidewalk along the Mississippi. How could anybody seriously think I had murdered Sunday Parker? Maybe Ash was right. Maybe I should go someplace new. Be someone new. Maybe Ash would even see me in a different way, maybe the way I wanted her to see me.

Maybe, maybe, maybe. A fresh start.

"You can't leave," a voice said.

Loud and soft at the same time. It seemed to come from the river, like the river was talking directly to me. I loved the river, the idea of it stretching all the way from the top of the country to the bottom. Over two thousand miles. Over a mile wide in places. It was a monster. The king of rivers. Gram had once told me that the river sometimes whispered things to those who could hear when they passed, but I'd never heard a peep from it before.

I skidded to a stop. I listened. I wanted to hear more and I didn't want to hear more. What did it mean? I sat on my bike hoping for some explanation. All I heard was what was already in my mind. *You can't leave.*

25

As soon as I pulled my bike into the driveway, I heard an engine start nearby. I turned and saw a Toyota across the street, the driver's-side window rolled down.

"Jack Bell," the driver called.

I walked over to the car, and as I got closer I realized Alice's roommate, Harmony, was in the driver's seat. My first thought was *Christ, no, not another dead girl.* I felt a chill as I got closer. But then I relaxed: she didn't have dead-girl eyes and she was driving. The dead don't drive.

"I'm leaving Nirvana," she said. I noticed right away that she didn't give me the Nirvana-ite greeting, which was strange. They always gave the greeting *Namaste. Don't do drugs. Life is magic.*

"Are you OK?" I said. Her eyes were all puffy and red, and mascara was clumped beneath them.

"Not really," she said.

"Do you want to come in?"

"I did something wrong. I'm going to tell you, and then I'm going to drive away. I'm never coming back. I always liked Brandon. Really liked him. Then Alice started acting so strange and he was confiding in me, and one night we kissed. And I went for it. I told him about my feelings. I told him everything."

"And?"

"He turned me down. He said he loved Alice. There's no way he pushed her unless he wasn't himself. Even then I don't believe it."

"How could he not be himself?"

"The professors, His Holiness, all of them. They make the Nirvana-ites think they experience otherworldly things. They have these meetings. They have them all the time. A professor leads them. You have to attend at least one every month. They convince you that you need to. They make you believe you experience what everyone comes to Nirvana to experience. Visits to another world. Spiritual clarity. We were all at a meeting that night. The night Alice died."

"And you experienced something?"

"Professor Weingarde was leading it, but he had to leave early. It's one of the rules that a faculty member is always there for a meeting. Occasionally someone has a bad experience in another world. The professor talks them through it. Gets help if needed."

"But you said he had to leave."

"And Alice had a bad experience. She started screaming at Brandon and me. She said she saw that we were
hooking up behind her back. I started having a bad experience because I felt so guilty. I had to get out of there.
That's why I wasn't there when it happened."

"You think she hurt herself?"

"We take oaths not to talk about these meetings. We
sign things. They say it's to protect us, but it's to protect
them. Find out what happens at those meetings."

"Tell me."

"I can't," she said. "I'm afraid. They know I talked to
you before. I can't tell you any more. I'm afraid of what
they might do."

Her dark window slid up.

"What happens?" I shouted, but she was already
driving away, and she kept driving.

There was no way those Nirvana students were going
to the spirit world. So where were they going?

When I finally went to bed, I had a bad night. It was
one of those nights when you keep having the same
dream over and over again and it never seems right and
you never get to the end of it.

How wasn't he himself?

What happened—or didn't happen—at those
meetings?

What did the river mean, I couldn't leave?

26

The next morning Mom, Amanda, and I were having breakfast together when someone knocked on the door. I was spooning Frosted Flakes into my mouth, and Mom was putting a scrambled egg and a piece of toast in front of Amanda. Dad was up and gone to the bar/café for his morning shift.

"You two eat," Mom said, and went to the door.

I could hear the breathy catch in our mother's voice as she said hello and then some hesitant conversation — with a man. Then I recognized his voice.

I looked at Amanda, but she was busy doing that thing she did with her scrambled eggs before she ate them, piling them into a pyramid shape or whatever.

After about a minute, Detective Bloodsmith came into the kitchen, wearing the same suit he'd worn the night he'd caught me in Alice's dorm room. Different tie, though.

"Good morning," he said, as if we weren't mortal enemies.

I said a begrudging good morning back. I watched him closely, like a dog I didn't trust.

Mom poured him coffee in one of my dad's mugs, which was just totally wrong. I almost said something smart and cutting, but I couldn't think of something smart and cutting, so I kept quiet.

"I'm Amanda," Amanda said.

"Yes," Mom said, like she was confirming something she'd forgotten "This is my daughter, Amanda, and my son—well, you've met my son."

"Oh, yes," Detective Bloodsmith said. "I've met Jack quite a bit lately. But Amanda, it's nice to meet you."

Amanda eyed Bloodsmith suspiciously. "My brother didn't kill anyone. He believes in Mahatma Gandhi's principles of nonviolence."

Somehow she knew what she wasn't supposed to know. My little sister's gifts—or curses, depending on your point of view—were getting stronger.

"I'm glad to hear it."

"My dad does, too," she said, and stressed the word *dad*.

I wanted to kiss her for that.

"Amanda," Mom said.

"They're good principles," Detective Bloodsmith said,

an uncomfortable smile on his rough face that made me feel a little more comfortable.

"So how have you been, Michael?" Mom asked.

Michael. Ha! The detective blushed a little. He looked almost boyish.

"Mike," he said. "I go by Mike now."

My mom didn't care for nicknames. I could have told him that she wasn't going to ever call him Mike even before she repeated, "So how have you been, Michael?"

He sat back and smiled slightly. He was not a big smiler like my dad, but I didn't hold that against him. Most everything else, but not that.

"Same old Claire."

"Afraid not," she said, and nodded toward Amanda and me as if we were her evidence.

This seemed to remind him why he had come.

"I need to talk to your son, Claire. I have more questions."

"I've been advised to get a lawyer," Mom said.

"If the boy has nothing to hide, why do you need an expensive lawyer?"

"He has nothing to hide."

"I hope so, for your sake."

"This shouldn't be the first time you come to my house after all these years. We said we'd stay friends."

"You said that," he said, and then he took a sip of his coffee. He looked like he'd swallowed pieces of glass. I saw something with my third eye—him standing by the river. Not him. A young him. He was crying. I turned away from that image as quickly as I could. Too often I saw things I didn't want to see with my third eye. Just then it definitely seemed more curse than gift.

"Well," she said, "that's the past. I heard you got married."

"I did. Didn't take, though. I have a little girl out of it. She's about the age of your girl here."

"It's a nice age," Mom said.

I was about to gag over all this polite conversation. Amanda's lip had set into that pout my mother worried would be permanent.

"I've got to go to school," I said.

"If it's OK with your mom," Detective Bloodsmith said, "I'll drive you."

Just what I wanted, to pull up to school in a detective's car. There didn't seem to be any alternative, though, and at least I'd get him away from the house and Mom.

"May I have a private moment with you, Michael," Mom said, "before you take him?"

They went into another room. Amanda was staring at her pyramid of eggs.

"You should eat those."

"I might go on a hunger strike like Gandhi did," she said. "I might not eat anything until everything goes back to how it was before."

I knew what she meant. But I also knew there was no going back. It made me feel different, older, I guess, to know this.

"You're not going to eat anything? Not even chocolate?"

She looked torn. She thought it over. "Maybe I'll just eat chocolate. Maybe my hunger strike will be everything but chocolate."

When Mom and Bloodsmith came back, the detective's face was bright red—but this time it wasn't embarrassment. Mom looked triumphant.

"Have a nice day at school," Mom said to me.

"Come on," Bloodsmith growled, and headed outside without waiting for me.

I looked at my mom, who shrugged.

Bloodsmith had hardly pulled the car away from the curb before he growled some more. "I guess you know about your mom and me."

"I didn't," I said, "until after you arrested me."

"It won't influence the case. I won't listen to cockamamy stories. I look at the facts and that's what I go by. Facts. Nothing but the facts."

This sounded like it might be from some movie, but I couldn't think which one.

"OK, Michael," I said.

He stopped the car. "You call me that again and I'll knock your head off. You hear me, kid? And don't try telling me you talk to dead people."

"I won't," I said.

"But you think you do."

"You just told me not to try telling you that."

"I'd advise you not to try that in court if this comes to court. I promise you it won't end well. Even in this crazy town, it won't end well."

"What did you want to ask me?"

He didn't seem to hear me. "We might as well be living in the Middle Ages if we believe in the things some people in this town believe in."

I understood his point. I mean, if I didn't know what I knew, I wouldn't believe in them, either.

"We're almost to school," I said. "You'd better ask me what you wanted to ask me."

He sighed and shook his head. "You look a lot like your mom. I didn't notice how much before."

"You knew who I was, though," I said. "When you arrested me, I mean."

"It's a small town. I missed that when I was in Chicago, and now I miss the anonymity of the city."

"Why'd you leave?"

He looked like he was about to answer but then said, "Never mind. You're the link, Jack. No matter how I look at this, you're the link."

"To what?"

"Not what. Who. Both girls. You were in Alice's dorm, and you discovered the Parker girl. She called you. She texted you. And she did it on the night she was killed. I have two murders and one boy who is connected to both girls."

"I didn't know Sunday Parker very well, and I didn't know Alice at all when she was alive."

He glared at me. I shrugged. I hadn't meant to say it, but now that I had, I wasn't sorry.

"What about Sunday Parker? She was alive when she called and texted you. If you didn't know her very well, why you? You still haven't answered that."

"I don't know why," I said honestly. "Maybe she thought I could help."

"Help what?"

I shrugged.

"I know you're lying about something. That I know. Some of her friends think this girl, Sunday Parker, was in some kind of secret relationship. You were the last person she called. Makes sense it was you."

"It does, but it wasn't."

"Why did she call and text *you*? The truth."

I wanted to do a Jack Nicholson imitation and say, "You can't handle the truth." (See *A Few Good Men*, 1992; writer: Aaron Sorkin; stars: Tom Cruise, Jack Nicholson, Demi Moore)

Instead, I just went ahead and gave it to him. "She was dying, and she thought of me. Not because we were together but because she thought I could talk to the dead."

Bloodsmith pulled up to the front walk of the school. Students were heading up the lawn. Some looked back to see who was going to get out of the sedan. The windows were tinted, so they wouldn't have been able to see well, but some would know anyway, the way some knew things. A detective had let Jack Bell off in front of the school this morning. Like the wind, it would spread around school. More bad gossip.

"That's not funny," he said.

"Let me ask you this," I said. "Why would I keep a relationship with Sunday Parker, a hot cheerleader, secret from my friends?"

"Maybe she wanted it kept secret. Maybe she was afraid of what her parents would say. You're not exactly what parents would desire in a boyfriend—especially Sunday Parker's. So you did it for her. You're a gentleman."

"I guess that's logical," I said.

He stared at me. He had a flat stare. It didn't give anything away, but it invited you to.

"If I was writing a movie," I said, "I might get by with it. I mean as motivation. Pretty weak, though. It'd be better if her parents hated my parents. Get a little Romeo and Juliet thing going."

"This isn't a movie," he said. "You can tell the difference, can't you, Jack, between reality and a movie?"

"Most of the time," I said.

"Working on some kind of insanity defense?" he said.

"You know Utopia isn't like other towns. You know that."

"Let's just be straight with each other. You were having a relationship with Sunday Parker, weren't you?"

"No."

"But you just said—"

"It might work if this was a bad movie, but it isn't true. Sorry. No."

"She was a beautiful girl. Corn Queen."

"Runner-up," I said.

"She texted you. She wrote 'life or death.' Explain that part to me."

Cops were repetitive.

"I explained," I said. "You won't listen."

"You might as well tell me that the world is flat."

"You grew up here. You were my mom's boyfriend. You probably know Gram. I know you know. You're the one who's acting like the world is flat."

"When I was in Chicago, I thought this town might have changed. We have the Internet, for God's sake. It hasn't, though. If anything, it's worse. We're going to be talking again. We're going to have a lot to talk about until you tell me what I want to know."

He told me to get the hell out.

As I walked up to school, my phone rang.

"This is your grandmother," Gram announced, as she always did.

"I wouldn't have recognized your voice," I said.

"I'm finally prepared," she said. "Took longer than I

thought. I'm off to the spirit world tonight. Midnight. You coming over or not?"

"Of course I am."

"Don't be late," she said. "Witching hour and all that."

Mr. Van Horn was on his toes a lot that morning in class. He was excited about the part of *The Great Gatsby* where Gatsby and Daisy are in love again. He wanted to discuss the difference between the love they felt now and the love they remembered. He wanted someone to explain to him why they couldn't get back to that earlier love.

I kept thinking about my parents. I knew they'd been in love. I knew from all the things they'd said and the way they really kissed and the way they talked. But lately it seemed like other things got in their way, and that made me wonder if other things had been getting in the way for a long time.

One time I sat with Mom on the sofa after Amanda and Dad had gone to bed. This was before he'd bought his bar. She'd drunk too much wine and she started describing how crazy she'd been about my dad in high school and how cool he'd been.

"He just had something," she'd said. "He was a beautiful boy and he had something beautiful. And he was all mine."

"He still is," I'd said.

She'd laughed in a way that wasn't a laugh and that made me uneasy. Then she'd said, "It was perfect. For just a moment, maybe. I hope you have that someday, Jack. Not many people do, you know. It was perfect."

Mr. White's history class was about the roaring twenties, which was the time of *The Great Gatsby*, flappers, and Prohibition. The Rasta Jocks managed to get Mr. White off the 1920s to Watergate (connecting the corruption of the twenties to the corruption in Watergate), and most of the hour was spent on this topic, which, as the twins knew, wouldn't be on the first test.

At lunch I finally found the person I'd been keeping an eye out for all morning, Eric Flute. He was sitting on the steps of the main staircase, which was where some of the jocks liked to sit. Two of his friends were with him, so I couldn't talk to him right away. I had to wait until the bell rang and he walked off down the hall alone. I hurried after him.

"I know about you and Sunday Parker," I said softly.

He looked at me like I was a bug he was about to squash.

"You're the one who found her," he said. "I heard the police think you killed her."

"I haven't told them that I know you and she were hooking up. Yet."

He was about six-two, almost two hundred pounds, and fond of stuffing freshmen in trash cans. A good old-fashioned bully. He stopped and shoved me up against a locker.

He whispered, "I know about you, Bell. My dad and I know. You're one of the freaks. You stay out of my head."

"I'm not one of those freaks," I said. "I can't read thoughts."

"Just stay away from me."

He let me go and we started walking. We passed people in the hallway. Some eyes lingered on us. We weren't two people normally seen talking to each other.

"How'd you know, then?" he said. "How'd you know about Sunday?"

"I didn't say I wasn't a freak. Just not the mind-reader type."

He gave me a hard stare. "I'm getting a football scholarship to Alaska. That was the farthest away I could get. I'm getting out of here and I'm never coming back. You freaks. You make me sick. What do you want, Bell?"

"Information."

We went up the stairs at the end of the hall.

"What kind of information?" he said.

"Did you see her that night?"

"She was supposed to come over, but she never made it."

"How long had you two been seeing each other?"

"Three months. It wasn't anything. Just sex."

"What about Emily?"

"It wasn't a big deal."

To him, I thought. But maybe it was a big deal to someone.

"Could Emily have known?"

"No," he said. "We were careful."

But then I saw something with my third eye.

It was the two of them in a car. Eric was letting Emily out somewhere. She said, "Don't call me. Don't text me. Leave me alone."

"She broke up with you," I said. "Emily broke up with you."

He balled his fists, which in the bully primate was a pretty clear sign that an attack was imminent. "I thought you said you couldn't—you weren't that kind of freak."

"I'm not," I said quickly. "I can see it by the way you look."

"We aren't breaking up. She's just upset. Sunday was her best friend. All right. I told you. Now you keep your end of the deal."

He was already in the classroom before I could point out that I hadn't actually promised him anything.

I looked for Emily between classes. No luck. I saw one of her friends, Megan somebody. I asked her if she'd seen Emily, and she said she hadn't come to school.

"You know Sunday Parker was her best friend," Megan said.

"I know."

"They say you found her," she said. "Her body."

"Yeah."

"Who would kill Sunday?"

At least she didn't seem to think it had been me.

"I don't know," I said.

"Emily is a good person," Megan said.

Something about the way she said this made me think she didn't think the same of Sunday Parker.

After my afternoon classes I went to detention. Mrs. Archer asked me how I felt about Sunday Parker's death. I told her I didn't feel like talking about it.

"It won't go away just because you don't talk about it."

"I still don't feel like talking about it."

Cassandra (goth girl) didn't feel like talking about it, either.

Mrs. Archer was kind of put out by this. There was a rumor that Mrs. Archer had been through a lot of therapy. I suppose she wanted to use some of what she'd learned.

To be polite I said, "I might want to write a screenplay about how I feel someday. That's how I work through my feelings."

"I'd like to see it."

"I'll let you know."

"Why don't you tell us what you're writing now, then?" she said.

I couldn't tell if she was calling me out or was interested. Either way I felt the need—for some reason—to tell her something. So I did a shameful thing: I stole the story from *Zombieland* (2009; writers: Rhett Reese, Paul Wernick; stars: Jesse Eisenberg, Emma Stone, Woody Harrelson). I'd seen the movie recently, so

I gave her a pretty good summary. Mrs. Archer wasn't all that impressed, but at least she didn't recognize the plagiarism.

Cassandra and I walked out together.

"Nice rip-off of *Zombieland*," she said.

"Ah, thanks," I said. "I was worried. Right after I started I thought maybe I should have done *Warm Bodies* instead," (2013; writers: Jonathan Levine, Isaac Marion; stars: Nicholas Hoult, Teresa Palmer, John Malkovich) "but—"

"You made the right choice," she said.

"Thanks for not telling."

"You got us away from counseling. Third teacher today who wanted to talk about Sunday Parker. I didn't even know her. And I thought she was a total idiot."

I didn't say anything. Seemed a bit harsh given the circumstances, but the truth was I'd pretty much thought the same thing.

She asked me if Ash was my girlfriend.

"No," I said.

"I thought she was—Anyway, I'm going to hear her tonight."

Then I remembered that the band formerly known as Good Girls with Bad Intentions and now known as Bad Girls with Good Intentions was playing at the Red Lion that night. I'd completely forgotten that I'd promised to go.

"I'll probably go," I said. "They're good."

"Cool," she said.

She stopped, so I stopped, and we stood in one of

those uncomfortable silences. Then I said, "Well, I'll see you later."

"Do you really see dead people?" she blurted out.

So that was it. She wasn't drawn to my magnetic charm or curious about my recent discovery of Sunday Parker's body. "Who told you I could see dead people?"

"Do you?"

"Do *you*?" I said.

"I've tried," she said, "but all I ever see are little streaks of light. But my grandmother saw them when she was alive."

"Maybe you're the lucky one," I couldn't help pointing out.

"It's a gift."

"Or curse," I said, "depending on your point of view."

Cassandra was short and very pale, though this might have been makeup. She'd be easy to mistake for dead on a dark night.

"You see them, don't you?" she said.

"No," I said.

I headed toward the bike rack. When I looked back, she was still watching me. As I unlocked my bike, I had this feeling that her asking about the dead meant something. Then I began to worry about what it might mean. I'd talked to two murdered girls in the past week and neither could remember how they'd been murdered. I turned back to Cassandra to say something to her — warn her, even if I didn't know exactly what I was warning her about — but she was gone.

27

I knew it was a bad decision to ride up to Nirvana College and to talk to Professor Weingarde. I knew I was risking more than a potential scholarship by going to see him. I went anyway. Harmony wouldn't have driven to my house and waited for me on her way out of town unless she thought she had something important to tell me.

Professor Weingarde's office was on the third floor of the Psychic Arts building, where a lot of professors' offices were. I was lucky to catch him as he was coming out the door. He looked a little like Principal Thompson. Tall, thin, rounded shoulders, tufts of white hair along with bald spots and a thin white beard that was aiming for Dumbledore but didn't come close.

"I don't know which class of mine you're in, young man," he said, "but pay attention to office hours. Time's over. On your way, now. And, you know, *namaste*. Don't do drugs. Life is magic."

"I'm not one of your students," I said.

He looked at me more closely. Then he asked me a strange question. "We aren't related, are we?"

"No," I said.

He looked relieved. "Well, then, you're too late, whoever you are. Office hours are office hours. I'm done for the day."

"I'm here about Alice and Brandon."

He tugged on his beard and cleared his throat.

"I have so many students," he said. "Can't say who you mean right off hand. Anyway, I have to be going now. I have some counseling to do with dead people."

He started down the hall at a good clip, but I was pretty sure I could outrun the old guy if it came to it.

"Maybe one of them is Alice."

"No, no," he said. "No, no. Afraid not."

Alice appeared now in the hallway, looking confused. I stopped.

"Professor Weingarde?" she said.

He didn't hear her or see her. He kept at his hurried march down the hall. I hurried after him, and Alice hurried after me.

"Professor Weingarde," she said again.

"He can't hear you," I said.

"What's that?" Professor Weingarde said.

"You can't hear her, can you?"

"Who?" The old man stopped and looked at me. "Who's here? I feel someone. Yes. Someone from the other side."

"Alice," I said.

"She's here?" His face looked a little white. His small eyes looked nervously at the exits. "You can see her? Now?"

"Are you all fakes here? Harmony said you were."

"Harmony," he said, standing a little straighter. "You've been talking to the wrong people. I can't talk to you now."

"She's angry," I said. "Alice is very angry at you."

His face got pale again. He tugged on his beard. "At me? It wasn't my fault. Tell her. I didn't mean for anything to happen."

"She can hear you. And she's very angry. If she touches you—"

I didn't finish because I didn't have a good threat. But just the suggestion seemed to do the job.

"I'm not angry," Alice said.

"Very angry," I said. "Sparks are flying off her."

"No, they're not," she said.

"She blames you," I said. "For the meeting. You know what I'm talking about. She blames you. She could reach into you and stop your heart. Ghosts can do that."

I was good. I almost believed myself.

"No, I can't," Alice said. "Stop saying those things."

"She's reaching for you, Doctor."

"I'm sorry, Alice," he said, his voice trembling. "The spiritual enhancer has never had that kind of effect on a student of mine. I'm sorry I couldn't help you."

"Spiritual enhancer?" I said.

He looked like he felt Alice's cold hands close to his heart. "I'm sorry." Then he made a run for it. He banged out the exit door. He moved pretty fast for an old guy.

"What was he talking about?" I asked Alice. "Spiritual enhancer—what's that?"

"For the meetings. Rituals."

"A drug?"

"They call it a spiritual enhancer. I've heard students call it the Other Side. It's used to enhance our spiritual journeys."

"You used it that night, didn't you?"

She was starting to fade. "I used it a lot of nights. We all did. I remember now! Brandon and I had a fight. I was screaming something all confused. It was me, but it wasn't me. What was I screaming? Something. It's all mixed up."

"So you and Brandon did have a fight."

"Yes. No. Not *us*. It wasn't us." She smiled a little. A sad smile. "I understand now. Thank you, Jack."

"I don't understand," I complained.

"It wasn't us," she said.

The air was rippling around her. Then I saw it begin to rip open, and I knew she was going and wouldn't be back.

"But who killed you?" I shouted, because the rippling was loud, wind whipping at me from all directions.

"I understand now."

I shouted, "Who killed you, Alice?"

"No one. No one killed me."

And she was yanked through the tear in the air and a second later she was gone. The wind was gone with her. I stood there, alone, the world around me silent.

28

On my way home, I went past the Bad Brew coffeehouse on the off chance I'd see Ash there. I looked in the window and didn't see her — but did see something. I almost went in, but I rode off instead. I rode fast. I wasn't trying to get away. Yes, I was.

I rode the long way home, down by the river, the image of my mom and Detective Bloodsmith sitting at the table drinking coffee together burning in my mind.

They had been sitting at one of the small tables, the kind for just two people, round so the chairs could be pushed together. They were leaning toward each other and my mother was saying something and he was listening intently.

I stopped in the park and sat on my bike, watching the mighty river make its slow and steady way past, and I cursed my mother. How could she go out with Bloodsmith? What were they talking about so intently?

"Talk to me, River," I said. "Help me out."

I sounded a little like I was praying, which was disturbing. The river didn't say anything back. I sat there for a while. I tried to see Mom and Bloodsmith with my third eye, then I tried not to. Then I rode home. I was disoriented, like you are sometimes when you wake from a bad dream. Only I wasn't waking from a dream.

Dad and Amanda were in the living room playing Monopoly, which Dad said was a crass game of capitalism that stood for everything he deplored but that he nevertheless enjoyed for reasons beyond him.

Amanda said, "You're late."

"Detention," I reminded her.

"You're still late," she said.

I put my hand on Dad's shoulder. "How are you doing?"

He looked a little confused but shrugged and said, "I'm fine. I'm worried about you. Other than that I'm good."

"Don't worry about me."

"I want you to stay out of all this now," Dad said. "No more talking to dead girls. Something is wrong here. Even I feel it. And I don't trust Bloodsmith to do the right thing. And—I'm worried."

"He says he just follows the facts."

"They just happen to lead to my son. I don't think so."

They did—sort of. I mean, I was at both crime scenes. I was the one connected to both dead girls. As they say in the cop shows, I looked good for it. But there was some other connection. I felt it. I just couldn't see it.

"Bloodsmith's not my problem," I said. I meant *not only my problem*. I meant *less my problem than yours*.

"He's your problem, all right," Dad said.

Dad rolled the dice and landed on Park Avenue, which would have been good, except that Amanda had a hotel on it.

"You owe me four hundred dollars," she said.

I went up to my room and texted Ash that my mother might be having an affair. I got a call about three minutes later.

"What are you talking about?"

I told her what I'd seen.

"You're kind of jumping to conclusions, aren't you?" she said.

"You didn't see them," I said. "My dad is going to be devastated."

"But there could be an explanation," she said. "You have to give her a chance to explain."

It all made sense now. My mother had started the arguments. She'd purposely trashed Jack Kerouac to get my father angry. Who would be next? Gandhi? Would she say all his talk about peace and love was a cover-up for his sexist attitudes to get my father in a state where she could pretend to be so upset she had to leave him?

"You don't really know anything yet," Ash said.

"You didn't see them." I saw them again with my third eye, leaning toward each other, alone together in that room of people.

"Just don't start acting all male and thinking you have to act when you don't know anything for sure yet."

I heard the screen door bang shut and Mom shouting she had pizza. My thought was she'd bought pizza as a bribe. She was trying to get Amanda and me to side with her on the divorce. Forget it.

"I've got to go," I said to Ash. "Anyway, could you quit telling me not to act all male? How else am I going to act? I am fricking male."

"I know," she said sympathetically, which made me angry. "Just don't act all stupid because of it."

I pressed the disconnect button on my phone. Then I realized I hadn't even gotten around to telling her about Alice and the professor and the drug they'd taken and what Alice had said: "No one killed me."

Served Ash right for acting all female. Ha.

I went downstairs. Everyone was in the kitchen by the time I got there. Plates were out; a pizza box was open. Mom and Dad seemed in good moods.

"Feeling guilty?" I said to my mother, and looked at her meaningfully.

"Guilty for what?" she said.

"For eating pizza," I said craftily. "All those calories."

"Your mom is the envy of all her friends," Dad said.

"But middle-aged people have to be careful," I said, thinking maybe that was it. Mom was having a midlife crisis. Maybe I shouldn't be so hard on her. This feeling was upended when I reminded myself that she was having an affair with the cop who was trying to arrest me for murder.

"You're acting a bit strange this evening," said the man who quoted Jack Kerouac, Gandhi, and Bruce Lee all the time.

"Am I?" I said.

"Yes," Amanda said.

"Must be my hormones. Teenager."

After dinner, we all played Monopoly for a while. My dad, the noncapitalist, was winning big-time when he had to quit to go to his bar. Up to that point, everything had been going pretty well. But Mom said something about him being able to stay home at night when he worked as a carpenter and furniture maker.

"I'm home almost as much as I was before," he said.

"But not at the same time as the rest of us. That's the difference."

"Just leave it alone, Claire."

But she couldn't. "And you made money."

Money. Money. Money.

That got them going. They snapped at each other. Dad's mouth hardened. Mom's eyes got watery. It ended, kind of predictably, with my father slamming the door when he left to go to work. Mom sat back in her chair, looking tired.

I remembered, and I wanted Mom to remember, this one time we'd watched *The Princess Bride* (1987; writer: William Goldman; stars: Cary Elwes, Mandy Patinkin, Robin Wright, Wallace Shawn, André the Giant), and she'd said that when they were young, Dad and she had been like Westley and Buttercup. They'd been separated, but their love had been strong, too strong to be truly separated. It had been a little embarrassing at the time to hear this, but now I wanted to remind her. Both my parents seemed to be suffering from amnesia. They were forgetting how much they meant to each other.

The fights were making them forget. Every day they remembered a little less. And I couldn't do a thing about it.

After a while Mom said, "Your father is bullheaded. He's all hippie-dippy go with the flow until he takes a stand, and then he is like a mule."

"Is he a bull or a mule?" I said. Maybe I wanted to fight then.

"He doesn't want to be a bartender," Amanda said.

"How do you know that?" I snapped.

"He should want to be a furniture maker," Mom said. "He makes beautiful furniture. It's art."

"Not that, either," Amanda said.

"What, then?" Mom said.

"Not a baris, a baris—"

"Barista," Mom said.

"Not that, either," Amanda said. "He told me when he was buying Madison Square Gardens."

"What does he want to be?" Mom said.

"He doesn't know."

Mom frowned, and I had to frown with her. I wanted to be on his side, but he was old. I mean, Dad was in his forties. He was too old not to know what he wanted to be.

"That's messed up," I said.

"I need a drink," Mom said.

Both my parents were abandoning me. That's how it felt. Why couldn't they act like they were supposed to?

"You need to go after him," I said.

"I so do not need to do that."

"But—"

"Just stop it, OK? You can't fix this, Jack. It's between your dad and me."

Mom told Amanda to get ready for bed and went to make herself a drink. A little later she reminded me that, having finally agreed I could be involved in Gram's trip, we had to be at Gram's at midnight.

Other grandsons took their grandmothers to church or brunch. I saw mine off to the spirit world.

"I'm going to go hear Ash play until I need to go. I'll meet you at Gram's."

"Where's she playing?"

"The Red Lion."

"It's a school night."

"I have to go to Gram's anyway."

She thought it over for a few seconds. "OK, but be on time."

I went outside to kill time before I left for the Red Lion. I saw the glow of Captain Pike's pipe from over on his porch. I remembered poor Lucy flying off toward the moon the night Sunday Parker was murdered.

"Captain," I said, "did Lucy come back?"

I heard Johnny Cash. He was singing about Folsom Prison.

"Nevermore," Captain Pike said. "She did her best to make it to the moon, but she's just a bird."

I said I was sorry. His pipe glowed orange. He blew out smoke. I saw it rise in the moonlight.

"I saw policemen talking about you today with my glass eye. You're a suspect in that high-school girl's death, too?"

"I'm very popular when it comes to the police. At least with one of the detectives."

"Your grandmother is going to the spirit world?"

His glass eye was very active. "Can you see if she's going to be OK?"

"I never can see much over there, but lately nothing at all."

"You know, I've never been sure what she means

when she says spirit world," I admitted. "I asked her, but she just said it's the 'other world.'"

"There's lots of other worlds. Seven seas. Five oceans. Other worlds. I've seen many in my time."

"But what kind of spirits?"

"Think of it like the animal kingdom of spirits. Does your grandmother have someone to help her? Is your mother going with her?"

"No one is going with her. I'm going to be there, though."

Captain Pike thought about this for a few seconds.

"I'm going with you," he said. "I feel great danger even if I can't see it."

"Really?" I said. "I'm not going to Gram's until midnight." Captain Pike went to bed pretty early. Like nine. "I'm about to head over to the Red Lion to hear my friend Ash play."

"Sounds good."

"It's a bar."

"I've been around the world five times. You think I don't know what a bar looks like?"

"Sure, but their music—"

"I think I've got at least one night in a bar left in me, boy. Anyway, she took my Lucy."

"She?" I said. "She who?"

"Never mind." He went inside to turn off Johnny.

When he came out, I asked him what he meant by

"she." He said I'd be the first to know when he figured that out.

"We'll take my car," he said.

His car was practically as old as he was. A hearse from the 1950s. Older than my dad. I had my doubts that it would even start, but it did. I wasn't sure if that was good or bad. He refused to let me drive. If I'd ever ridden with him before, I would have known better than to get in the passenger side, but I let my trusting nature get the best of me. I just had time to buckle my seatbelt as he backed off across his front lawn and bumped over the curb into the street.

The Red Lion was only two miles away, but in that short distance Captain Pike managed to run one of the few stoplights in town, scrape a parked car, wander over into the right lane (which was the wrong one for us), and force a bicyclist up onto the sidewalk.

When I got out, I kissed the ground—literally—which Captain Pike said was just plain overacting.

"I'm driving to my grandmother's or I'm walking," I told him.

"OK, maybe I'm a little out of practice. You can drive to your grandmother's provided you don't go above the speed limit."

I thought this was pretty funny, since he'd just broken about ten traffic laws, but I kept that to myself.

We went into the Red Lion. Captain Pike and I found bar stools. He ordered two whiskeys, Johnnie Walker

Black Label. The bartender wanted to see my ID, so I made a strategic switch to Coke.

The girls were already playing. Ash was singing and she nodded my way when she saw me. Captain Pike said they were good. "That little drummer girl really swings those sticks."

"That's Shelby," I said, watching her for a few seconds before I turned back to Ash.

I saw a few dead people in the bar but not Sunday Parker. None of these dead people tried to talk to me. Most likely they didn't see me. But the two murdered girls had seen me. They'd chosen me. I hadn't really thought of it that way before. Now that I did, it didn't seem like a coincidence.

I looked around and saw a girl who looked vaguely familiar sitting at the bar talking to a college boy (Nirvana students were usually pretty easy to spot). The girl was pretty, and I had this feeling I knew her, but I just couldn't remember from where. When she saw me looking at her, she lowered her face and turned so the boy blocked her.

"Do you know who that is?" I asked Captain Pike, who'd been around long enough to know practically everybody in Utopia.

He didn't even look. Maybe he saw her with his glass eye. "Elaine Harris."

That name was familiar. I was trying to remember someone from school and then I did—but it wasn't someone from school the way I'd thought. Elaine Harris had been my first-grade teacher. When she taught me, it was her last year before retiring. That was eleven years ago . . . which would make her in her seventies at least.

"Her granddaughter, you mean?"

"Afraid not."

No way. I went over to look at her. I couldn't believe how young she looked, how beautiful. I remembered her as a mass of wrinkles.

The boy with her was holding her hand, leaning in close to her, whispering something. He looked hopeful.

"Mrs. Harris?" I said.

The boy turned to look at me. He seemed confused about who I was talking to, but when he and I looked back at his date, we both got a surprise. Mrs. Harris's back had curved forward, her shoulders had dropped, her perky breasts had collapsed. She seemed thick in the wrong places. Even her pretty blue eyes had clouded and were hidden in folds of spotted, wrinkled skin.

The boy made a girlish squeal and practically fell off his barstool. Mrs. Harris reached for him, but he was too fast. He was out the door in seconds.

"You always were a disruptive boy," Mrs. Harris said, and slid stiffly off the barstool.

"I'm sorry," I said, trying to help her move through the crowd. "I didn't mean—"

She swatted me away, but I stayed by her. She seemed frail and unsteady on her feet. I opened the door for her.

"Disruptive. I remember. I was just having a little

fun, and you—you—" she said. Somehow she had a cane in her hand. She used it to give me one good swat on the knee and then she hobbled down the street.

I hobbled back to my stool.

"That hurt," I said to Captain Pike. Well, shouted. There was a lot of noise in the bar. The band. Voices.

Captain Pike said, "She's not the only old woman who uses her gift to sleep with young men. Must be quite a shock in the morning to the poor fellows."

"She looked so beautiful."

"They put a glamour on themselves." He looked around. "Don't see any others tonight, but they're out often enough. You'd better be careful who you go home with in this town."

I knew there were illusionists in Utopia. Like Mr. White had said, Utopia was once famous for its magicians. Those who had the gift—or curse, depending on your point of view—of illusion had often pretended to do tricks that were really magic. They made fortunes from their gifts. I suppose some of their descendants must still be around. Maybe Mrs. Harris was one of them.

I had to smile when I remembered the look on that college boy's face. Growing up in a town like Utopia did teach you one thing: many things are not what they seem. I was never surprised by being surprised.

When the band took a break, Ash and Shelby came up to the bar.

"You made it," Shelby said.

I introduced Shelby to Captain Pike. He knew everyone, so he probably knew her parents and he'd probably seen her around with his glass eye, but they'd never met. Ash had been over to my house many times, so he knew her.

The other girls in the band talked on their cells while Ash and Shelby told us how the crowd sucked tonight. They kept asking for country. Did they do Carrie Underwood? How about the Dixie Chicks?

"Somebody asked for Willie Nelson," Shelby said. "Do we look like we play Willie Nelson?"

Captain Pike smiled. His eyes were hard to see because of the folds of skin around them. He looked comfortable in the bar.

"You like Willie?" Ash asked Captain Pike.

"A true artist," Captain Pike said.

She nodded. "Yeah, he's cool. I don't want to play his music, but I like listening to it."

"Smart girl," he said, and winked at me with his good eye.

I touched Ash's arm. "Can I talk to you a minute?"

We went down to the other end of the bar and I told her about going back to Nirvana College and talking to Professor Weingarde and what Alice had said just before she moved on.

"Was it some kind of ceremonial drug? Is that what she's saying? I mean, it's not like heroin or crack, right?"

"She called it the Other Side. I don't know what it's

like. I googled it and nothing came up. But when your creed says, 'Don't do drugs,' it can't really be a drug, right?"

"You've got to tell somebody," she said.

"Who? And what would I tell them? I don't really know anything yet."

"Yet?" she said. "Stay out of it."

"I'd like to, but I'm already in."

"Don't you have enough to worry about? Don't you feel alive enough now?"

"It's not like that. If they give the students drugs and that girl killed herself, then they're at least partly to blame."

She frowned. She looked like I felt: conflicted. "Just be careful."

We went back over to the others, and Ash said she was going to talk to Nathaniel, who was at a table with other guys dressed in black and smoking e-cigarettes. Shelby stayed behind, but the other girls followed. Captain Pike began talking to a woman who sat to his right. He winked at me again.

"I'm glad you made it," Shelby said.

We talked. She said words. I said words. It seemed pretty easy. We even found we had something in common: we both disliked Nathaniel. We made fun of him. The break passed quickly. Soon the band was called back up onstage.

Shelby said, "So there's nothing, like, going on with you and Ash, right?"

"We're just friends. We've been friends forever."

"She's kind of possessive about you. I just said I'd like to get to know you better, and she started telling me all these things I should and shouldn't do. It was weird."

I felt my face coloring a little in the annoying way it did sometimes. "We're good friends. Best friends, I guess."

"Excuse me, but bullshit."

I planned on lying, like I always did about Ash, but I didn't. I'd reached my lying limit for the month. Or maybe Shelby made me want to tell the truth.

"It's bullshit," I said. "Sorry. It's all on my side, though. I'm trying to move on."

"You poor schmuck."

"Schmuck?"

"My dad's word. Look, I think you might be wrong about it all being on your side."

"Tell that to the boyfriend in black," I said, nodding toward Nathaniel, who seemed to be holding court at his table, though everyone looked a little bored by his court.

"Not for long, I'm guessing."

"There'll be another one waiting just around the next corner," I said.

She put her hand on my cheek and looked me in the eyes. She had awesome eyes. Green but blue too. She kissed me hard on the lips.

"It's too bad," she said, and she walked up to the stage.

It was too bad.

The band started playing. I ordered a Coke and whiskey without the whiskey and drank it down. Captain Pike stopped talking to the woman next to him and told me I was a damn fool and I agreed.

We listened to a few songs. Time moved close to midnight.

"You'd better drive," Captain Pike said, like we hadn't decided that before. He handed me the keys. "I've become a lightweight since I turned a hundred. More than five or six whiskeys and I'm unfit for the road."

"You couldn't be any more unfit than you were when you were sober," I said.

"Then I might as well drive," he said, reaching for the keys.

I held them away from him. "Don't even think about it, old man."

29

Gram looked relieved to see Captain Pike with me. It made me even less certain I should let her go. She invited us in and had us sit in the living room while she got Captain Pike more whiskey and me a beer. Gram had sort of a unique view of the law. She thought it should be followed when it made sense and ignored when it didn't. Lucky for me, she thought the minimum-age drinking law should be ignored.

"You don't have to do this, Gram," I said.

Gram said, "I made a potion to talk to Catherine."

Catherine was a spirit of some kind that my grandmother talked to from time to time to get information. She was a big gossip in the spirit world, apparently.

"What did she say?"

"The town is in more danger than it's ever been in. You're in more danger than anyone else. Then she disappeared. Very unlike her. That spirit loves to talk."

Gram's potions made her able to do many things besides just talk to spirits. She could make animals talk and make people appear to disappear, and she even made potions to change appearance, like Mrs. Thompson's glamour gift. She'd made a potion to take her to the spirit world.

"Maybe you could try calling her again," I said. "Maybe you wouldn't have to go to the spirit world if Catherine could tell you what the danger is."

"I don't think she knows. I think it scares her or embarrasses her that she doesn't," she said. She turned to Captain Pike. "I don't suppose you've been able to see anything more clearly than before?"

"Afraid not," Captain Pike said. "Like Catherine, I feel a great threat, though."

She shook her head. "The only way for me to know what kind of trouble is coming is to go to the spirit world. I have to get closer to whatever it is."

"Isn't there a potion for seeing farther?" I asked. I was less and less comfortable with her going there.

"I've tried that. Something is making it hard to see beyond this world."

"Yes," Captain Pike said. "Something very powerful. Very dangerous."

"That's why I have to go," she said.

"Isn't that why you *shouldn't* go?" I said.

"Believe me, I'll be in and out in a jiffy. No hanging around for tea. We need to know what we're up against. It's too dangerous not to go."

"Doesn't that mean it's too dangerous to go?" I said.

She stood and said, "Come here" to me, and she hugged me and told me to eat my vegetables and remember that I was a good person but could always be better.

"Where's Mom?" I said.

"Still sleeping," Captain Pike said, looking with his glass eye.

"I put a little something in her tea," Gram said. "I love my daughter, but she couldn't help with this. She'd just worry, and her worry can be very strong."

"Tell me about it." She was going to be something very different from worried when she found out Gram had drugged her.

"If something should happen and I can't return—"

I interrupted. "You better return."

"Yes, but if I don't. Just remember. You're going to do great things."

"Gram—"

"Now," she said. "Make me some tea, Jack. I'll be very thirsty when I get back."

I nodded.

"You're ready, then, Beverly?" Captain Pike asked.

"Let's do this," she said.

"Can I hold the door for you?" Captain Pike said.

"That would be gentlemanly of you," she said.

"What can I do?" I said.

"Make tea," Gram said. "We'll have more to talk about when I return."

"All right," I said. I didn't really have much choice. I thought I was going to be backup, but it looked like she preferred Captain Pike. I resented this a little. I was her grandson. At the same time I was relieved he was with us.

"It should just take a few seconds in this world," she said.

But she wasn't back in a few seconds. Or a few hours. She wasn't back at all.

The queen lives for a thousand years without finding him, and then she does. She hears the beating of his heart from hundreds of miles off and from the far greater distance of her prison.

Almost his heart.

She has learned to whisper in the world and to show herself for a few seconds at a time. A flicker of herself, but enough to see and be seen. She whispers to Joshua Bell, the descendant of her lover, more than a hundred generations removed, and brings him to the place where the city once was, and he builds the town of Utopia.

She seduces the short-liver and he, as Ishi had, falls in love with her. She does not allow herself to imagine for a second that he is Ishi. Once she has him, she digs her claws into him and rips his beating heart out of his chest. His screams excite her. She devours his heart. Nothing happens. Nothing.

Then something does.

The earth shakes. It splits open into jagged cracks that eat her slaves and animals. She curses the king. She curses the universe. Her curses cause even greater shaking and cracks. She almost slips into one herself. She must be calm. She fights the rage and calms herself and then calms her universe.

It was not close enough, she thinks. Not close enough to Ishi's heart. But there will be others, and she will find the one that unlocks the door.

Since that first Bell, she has visited three more in their

dreams and convinced them to sleepwalk to a place she can make them cross. Then she has taken their hearts. Then she has been disappointed.

Now there is another, one who seems closer to Ishi than all the others. But unlike the others, he somehow keeps her out of his dreams. She cannot make him sleepwalk to the crossing place. So far her other methods have failed.

And then the old witch comes to her, like a gift.

30

Here's what happened. Gram drank her potion and gave a few drops to Captain Pike. Then she whispered some words that I didn't understand. They sat on the sofa. They went into some kind of trance.

Gram and Captain Pike sat there in their trance for a long time—much longer than the few seconds Gram had promised—and eventually I felt hungry, so I went and got a bag of potato chips. I'd just sat back down in the armchair when something began pulling me. Not physically—not my body—but *me.* It pulled hard, and in that second the room changed and became a tunnel of sky. I was blown or pulled through it. I grabbed for something to hold, but the sides of the tunnel were clouds. My hands went right though them.

I saw Captain Pike in front of me, and I shouted at him. He was being pulled down the tunnel, too. At the very end of it I saw darkness. We were both going into the darkness. I caught up with Captain Pike and I tried to grab his arm, but he was just ahead of me. The air turned gray and then black. Just as we were going into the dark, Captain Pike's left arm swung forward almost like he was pitching a softball. A door I hadn't seen before slammed shut.

I was back in my chair.

Captain Pike's eyes opened and he shook awake, like a dog shaking water from its fur.

"Beverly?" he said, turning to Gram on the sofa.

"She's right here," I said, relieved.

But she wasn't. I saw that a second later. Her body was here, but Gram hadn't come back.

"I don't know where she went," he said.

"The spirit world." I wondered if the fall had confused him.

"Not the spirit world I know," he said. "We moved *through* the spirit world, maybe."

"No spirits?"

"One spirit. A monster. The monster grabbed her, and there was nothing that I could do about it."

It was true that from time to time our gifts — or curses, depending on your point of view — attracted monsters to our town. Gram had told me about one that she and her own mother slayed. It had been called from where it lived by a girl who expected to use the monster to hurt another girl she thought was bullying her. But once she'd called the monster, the girl couldn't control it. The monster was twenty feet tall, with claws as large and sharp as curved swords. It had three eyes. It breathed fire. It killed many people but only those with more good than bad in them. It planned to create an army of men and women with more bad than good in them and eventually a race of men and women with more bad than good in them. It was the Hitler of monsters. Gram tricked it into drinking one of her potions and sent it back to where it had come from.

That was a close one for the human race.

Some people didn't believe in monsters, but I wasn't one of those people.

"What kind of monster?" I asked Captain Pike.

"I can't say."

"A spirit?"

"Neither alive nor dead, Jack. That's all I could see."

"But Gram's alive?"

He nodded gravely. "Whatever it is, this monster, she's holding Beverly. I saw that. Female. The monster is female. She didn't kill Beverly. She wants something."

We tried to whisper Gram back into her body. Captain Pike reminded her that I was here. That we wanted her back. Captain Pike even tried some kind of calling spell he'd learned from a witch doctor on a small tropical island. Nothing worked. I called Mom, who was over in ten minutes, a sleepy Amanda with her. Mom settled Amanda in the guest room and then tried to wake Gram herself. She spoke to her. She asked her back. She even recited a spell Gram had taught her when Mom was young and Gram hoped she had a gift for spells or potions. She had neither. Mom could see and speak to the dead, but she had no gift for witchcraft.

"What was it?" Mom asked Captain Pike.

"A monster."

"What kind?"

Captain Pike shook his head. "It was like a rogue wave. Came out of nowhere."

"Mom is too old," my mother said. "Stubborn old witch." Then she teared up.

Captain Pike said thoughtfully, "This was no ordinary spirit. I'm not sure any mortal could have overpowered her."

"But Gram is alive," I said. "This monster has her, but she's alive."

"Yes," he said. "She's alive because the monster wants to use her."

"Use her for what?" Mom said.

"I'm not sure," Captain Pike said.

We laid Gram out on the sofa and got a pillow and

some blankets, and Mom shooed Captain Pike and me out the door, telling me to take Amanda home.

"I'll stay in case Gram wakes."

I think even then we knew she wouldn't, though. The monster had her.

31

The next morning Dad got up and had breakfast with Amanda and me, which just made everything seem more wrong somehow. He called and talked to Mom. He reported to us that there was no change in Gram.

"A monster's got her," Amanda said.

"You heard us talking," I said.

She shook her head. "Saw it in a dream," she said, and then she wanted her scrambled egg, which my dad attempted to make but made all wrong, according to Amanda. Too runny. Then he burned the toast. This led to uncharacteristic tears from my sister. We were all pretty upset.

Both Dad and I tried to console her, which did little good. She went upstairs to get dressed without eating much of anything. Also not like her. Most days she ate like a college football player.

"Can you take Amanda to school?" Dad asked.

I said I could. He was drinking a cup of coffee, but it wasn't doing much good. Dad had never been a morning person. I could see he just wanted to crawl back into bed.

"Did you tell Amanda you didn't know what you wanted to be?" I said.

"What?"

I repeated the question.

"That girl talks too much."

"She told Mom and me."

"Great," he said.

"That's exactly what I said. Great. My dad doesn't know what he wants to be."

"I'm going through something. I'm a little lost at the moment. No, not lost. At a loss."

"I'm the one who's supposed to be confused," I said. "Adolescence. Raging hormones. You're supposed to be guiding me."

"Do you need guidance?"

"Yes," I said. "Hell, yes."

"Ask away," he said, taking a drink of his coffee.

"Not right this second," I said. "In general."

"I'm sorry, Jack. I didn't plan this. I'm not happy about it. I guess we'll just have to be confused together."

Amanda happened in then and said we were going to be late for school. Dad insisted she take a granola bar for her breakfast, and we trudged out to my bike. Amanda ate her granola bar on the way. She had to ride on the handlebars, of course. She wanted to do the *Titanic* movie scene and hold her arms up in the air and scream like she was Kate Winslet hanging off the front of the ship.

"Not today," I said.

As I pulled up at Amanda's grammar school, she said, "The monster has Gram, but she wants you."

"How do you know that?"

"More of my dream," she said. "I remembered it when I was brushing my teeth. The monster wants you."

I asked her if she remembered anything else. She said she remembered that she was supposed to bring family pictures to school and she hadn't. I said I'd tell Mom. Maybe she could bring some by.

"Embarrassing," Amanda said, and skipped off.

I waited for her to get up to the door. Sometimes I wished I could be a little kid again. It wasn't like I hadn't had problems then, but they seemed to come one at a time and not from all directions.

I rode by Gram's on the way to school and found Mom asleep in the chair next to the sofa. I woke her, and she said she was going to make some oatmeal. When she found out I'd already eaten, she told me to go on to school. She told me she was going to stay with Gram for the day.

"I've called Dr. Hill," she said.

"What if he wants her to go to the hospital?"

"Maybe that's for the best. For all we know, she's had a stroke."

"You know she hasn't."

"I don't really know anything. That's the problem. That is the problem too often these days. I should have been with her when she — I should have been here."

"She put something in your tea to make you sleep," I said.

She frowned. "I told her I was going with her whether she liked it or not."

"I'm guessing not," I said.

"I can't believe she drugged me."

"We have to get her out of there," I said.

"We can't help her. We don't have the right gifts."

"Mom," I said, and I was about to tell her what Amanda had said, but she stopped me.

"There's nothing more you can do here, Jack. I need some time alone to think. You go on to school."

I felt helpless. I was helpless. I got on my bike and rode to school. On the way I got a text from Ash telling me to meet her at the smoking wall. When I got there, she was smoking furiously. As I came up she said, "So I hear you're going out with Shelby."

"No," I said.

"She said you were."

I had to smile. And also feel another twinge of regret at missing out on someone like Shelby.

"We're not going out."

"Good."

"Why is that good?"

"She isn't right for you. Too high maintenance."

"I don't know about that."

"Trust me. Anyway, she's not right in other ways."

I thought about this. "She's hot and smart and funny and kind, and she likes me. In what ways is she not right for me?"

"She just isn't. You need someone more like you."

"Like Nathaniel is like you? Like any of the guys you go out with are—?"

"I broke up with him last night."

"Really?" I said.

She nodded.

"Good. I mean—sorry."

She blew smoke at me.

"I thought you were going to quit."

"I am. This is my last cigarette. I'll never be able to blow smoke at you again."

"I'll miss it," I said.

"We were arguing about you. When we broke up. You and Shelby, anyway. You're right. I don't know what I was doing with him."

For one second I thought about asking her why she was so worried about me going out with Shelby and seeing if the conversation went anywhere. But then I thought about all that was going on in my life. I didn't need another disappointment. So instead I told her about Gram.

She listened closely. She liked Gram a lot. "We've got to do something," she said.

"Mom thinks she should go to the hospital. I'm not sure."

"It's like a coma?"

"Or a spell."

The bell rang. As we were walking up to school, Ash said, "Have you told the police about the drug that Alice and her boyfriend were taking?"

"Spiritual enhancer," I said. "Not yet."

"His Holiness knows about the spirit world. My mom says he does, anyway."

"Maybe," I said. I kind of doubted he knew anything, but he was a spiritual leader in Utopia and he did have some kind of power—even if it was maybe just a powerful voice.

"Maybe he can help us," she said.

"Why would he—?" But then I understood. Smart girl. "I tell him I won't talk to the police in exchange for him helping us get Gram back?"

"It's a thought," she said.

"A good one. Well, a good bad one, anyway. Not good for Alice's boyfriend, though."

"Not so good for him. Maybe we can find another way to help him."

The bell rang.

"I've got to go to class," Ash said. "We can think this out. We'll find a way to get her back."

I nodded; we'd always been good at thinking things out together. We walked into the school and she went down the hall and I went up the stairs to my class on the second floor. Sunday Parker blocked my way as I went down the hall, which was mostly deserted by then. She was wearing her cheerleading outfit but didn't look very cheery.

"I want to ask you to do one more thing for me. Just one more."

"The last favor I did for you almost got me put in prison," I pointed out. "It still may."

"Yeah, sorry about that."

I looked at her more closely. Her eyes. I saw it.

"You can go now, can't you?"

She nodded.

"How?" I said. "What happened?"

"Tell Emily I'm sorry. I'm really sorry."

"Tell Emily you're sorry for sleeping with her boyfriend?"

"Not that."

"Not that?"

"She'll know."

"She'll know? What about me? I need to know. Why can you leave all of a sudden? What did you find out? You know the cops still think I might have killed you."

Well, one cop.

"I could always go," she said. "I just needed to watch a little. I think I knew, but I needed to be sure."

"Watch what?"

"It needs to be now, Jack. Emily's at home and she's — she's thinking bad thoughts, dangerous thoughts. I need you to go now."

"First tell me who killed you."

"She's in trouble," she said, beginning to fade.

"Don't you dare," I said. I could hear it. The same rush of wind I'd heard when Alice was leaving.

"Who killed you?" I shouted.

But she was gone. Faster than Alice, even. There and then not.

I cursed and walked toward class, but before I got to the door, I turned around. I grumbled some more curses, but if what Sunday Parker had said was true — if Emily was in danger of hurting herself, maybe killing herself — I couldn't just ignore that. And the last thing I needed was a visit from another secretive dead girl.

I rode to Emily's house, which was in the new subdivision on the north end of town, the same subdivision where Sunday Parker lived — had lived. There weren't many houses in this area, only twenty-five or thirty, and they looked alike. Big, with stone fronts and wide lawns, all next to a country club with a golf course.

I parked my bike in Emily's driveway. It wasn't until then that I thought the thought I should have thought at school: What if Emily had done what Sunday Parker was worried she would do and she was dead? What if I was showing up at the house of another dead girl? I should hop right back on my bike and pedal off. But what if there was still time to stop Emily from hurting herself?

Crap.

Please don't be dead, I thought as I walked up the long sidewalk to the front porch. *Please don't be dead.* I knocked on the front door. To my immense relief, Emily answered, and while she didn't look much like the Emily who was always so put together—no makeup, her hair hanging in a droopy version of itself, her pink sweats stained with . . . I wasn't sure what, but it wasn't good: maybe chocolate—at least she was alive.

"Jack Bell," she said. "What are you doing here?"

"Can I come in?"

"I'm not—I'm not really seeing people."

"I need to talk to you."

She hadn't really looked at me until then. "Is this about Sunday?"

"Yes," I said.

She stared, and if I didn't know better—but actually, come to think of it, I didn't—I'd think she was reading my mind. "Maybe you'd better come in, then."

We went into the living room. Big, stately, expensive, ugly.

"You said you had something to tell me about Sunday," she said, sitting in an armchair and motioning for me to sit on the sofa.

"I talked to your boyfriend."

"Ex-boyfriend."

I remembered my vision about their fight. "You must have been pretty mad."

"At Eric?" She smiled. "The one silver lining to all of this? I don't have to go out with that jerk anymore. You talked to her, didn't you? Sunday. Before she died. What did she say about me?" She grabbed a tissue from a nearby box and wiped her eyes. That's when I noticed the pile of tissues by her chair.

"She said to tell you she was sorry."

"That's it?"

"She was worried about you."

She blew her nose and stood up, a not-so-subtle "it's time to go" message.

I had to try something more drastic. "I saw her after she died. She told me you were thinking about hurting yourself."

"I'm not."

"She was worried."

"Tell her to save her worry for herself. She's the dead one."

I did notice she wasn't questioning my talking to a dead Sunday Parker, which made me wonder if she came from a family with gifts—or curses, depending on your point of view.

"She slept with your boyfriend," I said. "That had to make you pretty angry."

"I hope she had a better time with him than I did."

"I'm sensing some bitterness," I said, but I wasn't sure what the bitterness was for.

She got out her phone and said, "I've had enough questions. Time for you to go. Or do I need to call the police?"

I definitely didn't need to see the police again. I left.

I got back to school in time for most of my second class. After lunch Ash texted me that she'd set up (through her mother, lawyer for Nirvana College) a meeting with the Cowboy Guru at his house for that afternoon. I asked her to meet me at the Bad Brew so we could go over together.

After my final class, I rode to the Bad Brew. I thought about Emily's bitterness as I rode. It wasn't for her ex-boyfriend. That's what I thought. Her boyfriend and best friend had betrayed her, but the bitterness was for Sunday Parker. Why?

I found a table by the big picture window and stared out at the street, which was empty except for a guy walking a golden retriever.

I thought about Gram and worried that she would never make it back. It was my fault. The monster wanted me, not her.

I had loved staying with Gram when I was little. She never wore shoes and she ran around her house like she was always in a hurry to get to the next moment. She cooked wonderful things. Soups. Desserts. Potions. These not only smelled good but filled the house with a special feeling, like more was somehow there than in other places. Her whole backyard was full of growing things, some of which were unusual: a talking sunflower (well, it said one word: "sun"), a yawning gigantic blue flower, and these tiny flowers with red tops that danced. Magic happened at her house. She could make things appear and disappear, but she always said these were just tricks and not real magic. Real magic changed things. Every once in a while she would show me real magic. I saw the difference. It made me see the world in a different way.

I wanted to learn to do magic, but while she could teach me the tricks, she couldn't teach me the magic. I didn't have the gift—or curse, depending on your point of view.

"Hello, Jack," my least favorite detective said, sitting down across from me.

"I'm meeting someone," I said.

"I'll move when she gets here."

I almost asked him how he knew it was a she, but I didn't want to extend our conversation.

"What do you want?" I said.

"Who says I want anything? Maybe I just want to say hi."

"Hi," I said. "See you."

A waitress brought him a tall beverage. "Compliments of the Bad Brew," she said.

"Thank you," he said.

"What's that?" I said.

"Double latte," he said, looking a little guilty. He put about six packets of sugar in it and shrugged. "I have a sweet tooth."

Since I had him answering questions, I tried to sneak in another one. "What did the diary say?"

"That's evidence," he said. "Anyway, no need for you to worry about that murder. We have a confession. Let's talk about the other murder."

"But you know he didn't do it, don't you?"

"I just follow the facts. There's no other suspect."

"But you know better. Your gut tells you, right? You're the kind of detective that listens to his gut."

"I follow the evidence," he said.

"You work from the gut, like John McClane." (See *Die Hard* 1–5, 1988–2013; writers: Roderick Thorp, various screenwriters; stars: Bruce Willis, various other actors.)

"You watch too many movies."

"Not possible."

"Until I find something that tells me he didn't do it, I have to work on the assumption that his confession is true."

"You can at least tell me what the diary said, right?

Because we both know it didn't say anything about me. If it did, you'd have me back in for questioning."

He took a drink of his latte.

"You know what quid pro quo means?" he said.

Thanks to *Silence of the Lambs* (1991; writers: Thomas Harris, Ted Tally; stars: Jodie Foster, Anthony Hopkins, Scott Glenn), I did. It's how Hannibal Lecter gets the agent, Clarice, to bargain with him.

"You give me something and I give you something," I said.

"Close enough," he said. "It was a normal college girl's diary. She was worried about her boyfriend, her grades, and her family. Normal Nirvana college girl's, I should say. She was worrying about failing her Communication with the Dead class."

"It's not as easy as people think," I said.

He frowned and took another drink of his latte. "But the last two entries were different. They didn't sound like the rest of the diary. Disjointed. The handwriting was even different. The first was just crazy stuff. It was almost like she was ordering herself to act. She wrote, *Find the boy. Find the boy.* It was written about a hundred times. The last entry got a little Edgar Allan Poe. It talked about smelling him and hearing the sound of his heart pumping blood through his body. It was as if someone else wrote those last few entries."

"Who?"

"Maybe the roommate."

"Why would she write in the diary?"

He shrugged. "My turn. Quid pro quo, remember? How did you find Sunday Parker?"

"She told me where to look."

He sat back and looked more sad than angry. "I thought we had an agreement."

"I'm not lying," I said. "Hook me up to a polygraph."

He waited, but I knew from cop shows that this was a detective technique. Be silent and let the perp (God, I was the perp) talk himself into trouble. Finally he said, "When she called, she told you where her killer would drop the body after he killed her?"

He was looking at me like he expected a lie. Maybe that was why I decided to tell him the truth. "She called and then texted, maybe as she was dying. I found her. Well, I found her ghost, anyway. She's the one who told me where her body was. Then she asked me to call you because she didn't want her body lying out like that."

"So we're back to you talking to the dead."

"Polygraph," I said.

"This town. This damn town."

"I think you should talk to Sunday Parker's best friend, Emily Fairfield," I said. I'd promised Eric I wouldn't say anything about him. I didn't promise his girlfriend I wouldn't.

"Why?"

"Ask her."

"Anything else?" he said.

"There is something but not about Sunday. Alice's roommate, Harmony, came to see me before she left town. She was pretty upset."

"She's gone?"

"Not coming back," I said.

"That's interesting."

"Did you know there was a meeting the night Alice died? Earlier Harmony was there and Brandon and Alice. One of their spiritual meetings."

"Something happen at this meeting?" Bloodsmith said.

"Alice accused Harmony and Brandon of hooking up. She was pretty upset."

"Were they?"

"No. But let's just say this was a movie and someone wanted to hide the fact that Alice killed herself. So this someone pressured Brandon to confess—which means the case doesn't go to trial. Then no one has to look too closely at the evidence against Brandon. No one has to look closely at the meeting either."

"This isn't a movie. Why would someone want all that?"

"Hiding something."

"What?"

I wanted to tell him, but if I did, I'd lose my chance to persuade His Holiness to help me with Gram. I knew a guy like the Cowboy Guru wouldn't help me if he thought I'd helped the police learn the truth about Nirvana College.

"I don't know," I said.

"This sounds like a movie again. Your overactive imagination." He frowned. "The facts point to the kid." He frowned some more.

"But . . ." I said. "Something feels wrong, doesn't it?"

His frown got even deeper.

"That's because something *is* wrong," I said.

"You know what still feels wrong to me? Still bothers me? You. You're the link to both girls. Why?"

"I don't know," I said. True, but he was looking at me like he was pretty sure it was a lie.

"You know what else I don't know?" I said. "I don't know why you and my mom were in here the other day having an intense conversation."

"We're old friends," he said.

"Is that all?"

"I'm not going to talk to you about your mom and me. Talk to your mom."

"I will."

"But I'll tell you this, Jack. If you're involved in these murders in any way—either murder—my feelings for your mother won't matter. I'll arrest you."

Just then, Ash came up to the table. "Sorry I'm late."

Bloodsmith, true to his word, got up. "I was just leaving. You kids have a good night."

"Who's he calling kids?" Ash said. "I'm going to get coffee. You want anything?"

I said I was fine. I wasn't, though. And not because of Bloodsmith's suspicions.

Ash came back with two lattes.

"What did he want?"

"Information."

"So did you give him any?"

"I told him that Emily knows something because Emily knows something."

"You said she broke up with Eric."

"Yeah. And guess what she said about it? She said that breaking up with him was the one silver lining to all of this."

"So why would she have stayed with Eric when she didn't even like him?" Ash said.

"I was wondering about that. I think maybe she was hoping to keep Sunday Parker from dating him."

"Why would she care?" Ash said.

"She didn't want them together."

"But if she didn't even like Eric, why would she care if Sunday dated him?" Ash said.

"Maybe she didn't want Sunday dating Eric because she didn't want Sunday dating anyone."

Ash raised her coffee cup to her lips but didn't drink. "You think Emily—?"

"Maybe."

"She loved Sunday Parker? Like, love-loved her?"

"If she did, then that, as they say, is motive."

"They who?"

"Movie cops and detectives. But think about it. Maybe Emily professes her love and Sunday Parker says 'I'm flattered, but . . . ' And Emily loses it. Maybe it was Emily's car she got into that night."

"It's possible," Ash said, not sounding very sure.

"I'm just saying it could have happened. Love is a powerful motive for murder."

"Kind of a cynical thought about love, isn't it, Jack?" she said. "At least Nathaniel was romantic."

"I can be romantic."

"Really?" she said. "Say something romantic."

"I have to be in the mood."

"That's what I thought."

"I could say something romantic, though. I mean, I could if I wanted to."

"Say it, then."

"Fine," I said. But if I did, then what? The truth would be all over my face, and where would we be with that truth?

"Forget it," she said.

Say it. Don't say it. Be smart. Go for it. Don't go for it. Don't be stupid. Do. Don't. My mind was full of contradictory voices.

I took a deep breath.

"I couldn't stop watching you that very first day we

met on the playground. We were ten. I couldn't stop watching you, but it wasn't because you were so cute, which you were, or so bossy, which you also were. It was because you did everything full speed. You didn't slow down for anything. I had to be close to you because you were so alive. It wasn't that I minded seeing dead people. I grew up with them. Mom saw them. Gram. But sometimes they seemed more real to me than the living. Not you. You were the most alive person I'd ever met. You still are."

Silence. Total silence. I think I might have closed my eyes or maybe it just felt that way. I looked at her. She was looking at me.

"That was — that was —"

I stood up because I was afraid of what she was going to say. "That was stupid." "That was nice but." I'd heard the *but* before, and I just couldn't take it now.

"Romantic," she said.

"Really? Even the dead people part?"

"Oh, yeah," she said. "Really. Even the dead people part."

32

Ash drove us over to the Cowboy Guru's house up on campus. Big. Square. Red brick. Stone gargoyles on the roof looking down at us. Ash parked in the circular drive, and we walked up to the stately front door, stained oak and stained glass. I rang the bell, which sounded like church bells. We were met by a stout gray-haired woman in a dress. She reminded me of Kathy Bates in *Misery* (1990; writers: Stephen King, William Goldman; stars: James Caan, Kathy Bates, Richard Farnsworth), which did nothing to make me feel less nervous. She led us through a huge living room back to a small study without saying a word.

The Cowboy Guru was sitting in his office. He got up when we came in.

"*Namaste.* Don't do drugs. Life is magic. So nice to see my two favorite would-be felons. Sit, please. Can

I have Mrs. Black get you something? Hot chocolate, maybe?"

We both said yes.

"Coffee for me," he told the Kathy-Bates-in-*Misery* look-alike. She walked out, slamming the door.

Both Ash and I jumped.

The Cowboy Guru apologized. "Big dinner tonight. She's always a little moody when she's cooking for a lot of people."

We did some small-talking about Ash's mom (one of His Holiness's favorite lawyers, he said) and my dad, who the Cowboy Guru had met at Field of Dreams once. Then he looked right at me. "I've been informed that you were informed about the . . . ceremony. Dr. Weingarde thinks you talked to the ghost of Alice and that she told you about the spiritual enhancer. I think it's more likely Alice's roommate, Harmony, talked to you about things she shouldn't have talked about."

I was about to tell him that it was the good Dr. Weingarde who'd told me, but just then the Kathy-Bates-in-*Misery* look-alike brought in the coffee and hot chocolate.

"Don't slam the door on the way out," the Cowboy Guru said. It was a quiet voice, but it didn't sound quiet. For just a second his eyes got cold and something cruel came into his face. It was like a mask dropped away for a second. He scared me.

"Yes, Your Holiness," she said. She hurried out of the room. She was scared, too.

The Cowboy Guru took a drink of his coffee and sat back in his chair. I looked around the room. Lots of crystals, glass sculptures, pictures of angels and demons and goddesses. The hot chocolate tasted very chocolaty.

"So," he said. "I think you may have gotten the wrong idea about our spiritual ceremonies."

"You mean the part about the professors giving the students drugs," I said. "Kind of undercuts the whole 'Don't do drugs' part of your creed, doesn't it?"

"It's not a drug," he said. "It's a spiritual enhancer. Very different."

"How's it different?" Ash said.

"Many cultures around the world use spiritual enhancers in their rituals. The use of ayahuasca in Amazonia and other places is but one example," he said.

"So the professors get the students high enough to think they really do have special powers," Ash said. "And the money from Mommy and Daddy keeps pouring in." She smiled after she said this.

His Holiness took another sip of his coffee. His body was taut. His eyes hard. "Most of our students come here expecting something profound to happen. They expect to be able to do magic, see visions, walk in the spirit world. But none of that can happen without help. So we help them. We have ceremonies. They experience something. We let the spiritual enhancers work. Are the students truly experiencing magic, seeing visions, walking in the spirit world, or just hallucinating? Who's to say?"

"I know which my money would be on," Ash said.

"No one is ever forced into anything. We are here to give spiritual guidance. *Namaste.* Don't do drugs. Life is magic."

"So people know they're taking a drug?" I said.

"*Spiritual enhancers,*" he snapped. "Their spiritual journeys are always supervised. We're very careful. That night was an exception. Professor Weingarde's daughter was in a car accident down in Iowa City. He had to leave class to go to her. Alice and Brandon became distraught in class. The other students said they got up and left together. The spiritual enhancer has never caused someone to act violently. I don't think this tragedy had anything to do with the enhancer."

He put his coffee cup back in the saucer.

"Alice said no one killed her," I said.

"Alice?" he said, and shook his head at me like I was being childish. "Let's just stick to what the living have to say. Witnesses heard her and her boyfriend arguing and things breaking. The next thing students in the dorm heard was Alice hitting the ground three stories down, her neck broken. Beyond that, I don't know what happened. So I leave it to the professionals. You should, too."

"Except you didn't leave it to the professionals. You had Professor Weingarde talk to Brandon. Make him think he killed Alice."

"Now, why would I do that?"

His voice was quiet, but there was a threat in it. He could make us disappear. Not with magic. With money. With knowing the right wrong people. I suppose this was my overactive imagination, but he was threatening.

"The drugs," I said. "If people knew you were giving the students here drugs—"

"Talk about a serious PR problem," Ash finished.

"So you have Brandon confess, and the police don't look into the whole story too closely," I said.

He let out a long sigh, as if we were exhausting him. "You two are going to be trouble for me, aren't you?" he said.

"I guess I can forget about the scholarship," I said.

"Not necessarily," he said. "Drop this ridiculous story about the drugs and the scholarship is yours. But if you choose to go to the police with this slanderous bit of fiction, then there's more you could lose, both of you, than just a scholarship. Think it over. Be the smart kids I know you are."

That was when I remembered about Gram. Not a very smart kid after all. There was no asking him for help now, but I was pretty sure he couldn't have given it anyway. Chris's mother was right. He didn't believe.

"You can leave now," he said. "*Namaste*. Don't do drugs. Life is magic."

We both got up and got out of there.

"He's going to let Brandon be locked up in some

psych ward or whatever so he and the school don't get bad publicity," I said once we were walking down the drive.

She nodded. "He's scary, isn't he? That quiet scary. Cold heart."

"Safe to say, he'll do some dark things to us if we get in his way," I said.

"But you're going to get in his way, aren't you?" she said.

"Probably."

As we were walking to the car, it just happened. We were holding hands. And when we got to the car, we kissed. I mean we really kissed. Full lips on lips, deep and soft. And again. All of this seemed natural, like we'd been doing it all our lives and always would do it.

Kissing her made me feel like I was floating in cool water on a hot, sunny day. But there was nervous energy crackling through me, too, like electricity sparking.

"I've got to get home," she said after a few minutes.

"Me, too."

But we kissed some more. Then we finally did get in the car, and when she let me off at the Bad Brew we kissed more. It was hard to stop.

On the way home, I kept thinking about how it felt to kiss Ash, about how it was both hot and cool at once, comfortable and strange; it almost made everything else, all the confusion and trouble in my life, fade away. Almost.

Dad greeted me as I came in the front door and told me about Gram.

"The doctor said stroke. An ambulance took her to the hospital in Dubuque. Your mom is with her."

"Can we see her?" I asked. So Dad drove Amanda and me to the hospital. We went up to the fifth floor, where the stroke patients were.

Amanda said, "Gram, you have to come back. You promised to show me how to skate on the river this winter."

I thought this was strange because no one skated on the river. The ice was untrustworthy, unpredictably thin in places. Gram had once said that witches might chance it because they wouldn't sink if they took the proper precautions, but as far as I knew, even she had never attempted it. Surely she wouldn't chance taking Amanda.

I debated telling Gram that I'd finally gotten that girlfriend she'd asked about, but then I realized I wasn't actually sure if Ash was now my girlfriend. Maybe what had happened had been a reaction to the crazy tension at the Cowboy Guru's place. Maybe she was already trying to forget it had ever happened.

When we left the hospital that night, Gram's condition wasn't one bit improved. Gram was trapped in a place beyond the spirit world, and we had no way of saving her. The doctors were convinced that she'd had a stroke and was now in a deep coma she would probably never come out of.

Dad talked Mom into coming home for the night. We were all exhausted. But with so many things on my mind, I didn't think I'd be able to go to sleep. I planned to just sit in front of the TV and try not to think. Mom and Dad and Amanda went upstairs to bed. I lay down on the sofa and I must have fallen asleep right away. I didn't even turn on the TV. It was a deep, deep sleep.

33

I had a dream in my deep sleep. I was in Utopia, but it wasn't my Utopia. The streets were dirt and no one was on them. A horse was tied up to a hitching post in front of a building. The sidewalks were wood and a couple of feet higher than the street. The buildings looked like they were from an old Western (See *High Noon,* 1952; writers: Carl Foreman, John W. Cunningham; stars: Gary Cooper, Grace Kelly). It was night but very light, and I looked up and saw a swollen moon.

A girl stepped out of the shadows. She had long white-blond hair and big eyes. She wore a long dress. It was the kind of dress that fit the time period of the town. She was beautiful, perfect, except her eyes were wrong. They were silver.

"I need you here with me, Jack Bell. Come to me, and your grandmother will be safe. Get up now and walk."

"Who are you?"

"Come with me now and I'll show you the way, and I will see that your grandmother returns safely to your world. Only you can save her. Don't you want to save her? And you will be happy with me. I will make you cry with joy."

She was beautiful. Crying with joy sounded—well, contradictory and complicated. I had the bad feeling there would be more crying than joy. But I knew she had Gram and I knew it was my fault she had Gram. So I got up. I walked.

Then I was down by the great river. It was flowing fast, a swirl of dark brown, little whirlpools spinning down and down. My third eye saw the brown water flow into the gulf hundreds of miles away and disappear in the oceans and seas. And I felt small and powerless.

Across the river, the white-haired girl rose into the air. She might have been wearing the same dress she wore in town at first, but as she rose I saw that she wore no clothes. I stared. Rude, maybe, but it wasn't a sight I was likely to see again. She moved over the water, and I could feel her hand touching my face even though she was far away. I could feel her mind in my mind—which I didn't like but couldn't stop.

"Your heart beats as his heart beat." She sounded satisfied.

"Whose heart?" I said.

"Cross the river," she said, "and I will show you. I will open your mind."

I saw a boat then, and a boatman behind a ship's wheel. The mist was thick, but I could see through it somehow. I heard the sound of water lapping against the boat.

"Come," the woman's voice said softly, and I knew I had to. I walked toward the bank as the ship came out of the mist.

Then I heard something from my childhood. It was my mother's voice. Like when I was a kid. She'd go out onto the front porch and shout my name. She was shouting my name then.

"No!" the girl with the white hair shouted. I saw her floating above the river. I saw her face angry and red. Her beautiful white hair became a nest of writhing snakes. I could hear them hissing. Striking blindly at the air.

I woke. The couch cushions were damp with sweat. It was dark in the room except for the moon coming in through the window. I felt a chill move through me. I had to get Gram back. I had to make the trade: me for Gram.

I tried to get back to sleep, back to the dream, but I couldn't settle down. I couldn't stop thinking of her hair becoming a nest of snakes and the rage in her swollen face. Eventually, though, I calmed myself and drifted away from the room and into sleep and dreams.

The queen thinks of Ishi as she is pulled back to her prison. The boy, the descendant, reminds her so much of him. She yearns to have Ishi's hand touch her, to feel his lips on hers, to lie with him. What madness is it that even more than a thousand years cannot kill?

Love.

Hate.

Love.

She considers keeping the boy for a time before eating his heart. He is so like Ishi. Even as she thinks this, she knows it is a bad idea. Better to cut out his heart and have a quick meal of it. Better to forget.

"Ishi," she says softly.

She loves him. She hates him. She loves him. Sometimes she is not sure who to blame for her prison: the king or Ishi.

She is sure of one thing, though: She is the last of her kind. She will be a goddess to the short-livers. They will worship her. They will have no choice.

34

I felt something shaking me and I opened my eyes and it was Mom standing over me. I couldn't remember my dreams after the one with the monster, but they hadn't been important. I sat up, disappointed. I was here. Gram was there.

Mom said, "I felt something in here when I came in. Was that dead girl here?"

"No," I said. "It was just a nightmare, I think."

Mom sat next to me and tried to put her arm around me, but I shrugged her off. She looked hurt.

"I saw you," I said. "With Detective Bloodsmith."

"You saw me doing what?"

"Ash says I should give you a chance to explain," I said.

"Does she? That's big of her. And you."

I felt a tiny crack in my righteousness but only a tiny one. "Do you have an explanation?"

She stood. "This isn't something I want to discuss with you."

She said she was going to make breakfast. She told me to go take a shower and wake my sister. I considered not doing what she ordered as an act of rebellion, but I did need a shower, and the bathroom was right next to Amanda's room. I took my shower and woke Amanda, who told me she'd dreamed Gram was stuck in a prison.

"She's in a hospital," I said.

"A prison," she said. "The monster."

"A white-haired girl?" I said.

"A monster," she said.

"You'd better get up."

"I could help you," Amanda said.

"Right," I said. "You could help me now by going down to breakfast. Mom's waiting."

She gave me a similar look to the one I imagined I'd given Mom when she ordered me to take a shower and wake Amanda, but in the end she made the same choice and did what she was told.

I dressed and went down to breakfast. Mom and Amanda were already eating.

"I just called the hospital," Mom said to me. "The

doctors are saying she's worse. They don't think she'll come back. They're talking about taking her off life support."

She started crying, and Amanda got out of her chair and hugged her. I'm ashamed to say I stayed in my chair.

Mom hugged Amanda and patted her on her back. She stood and went over to the sink and washed her face. Then she said, "I should never have let her make the trip. I knew she wasn't strong enough. I should have forced the issue—I've just been distracted by my own problems, by your father."

I didn't say, *And Bloodsmith. He distracted you, too, didn't he?* but I thought it.

"You can't let them take her off life support," I said.

"Your grandmother made a living will. Her wishes were very clear."

"You know she isn't in a coma. She's being held by that—that—"

"Monster," Amanda said.

"If we get her back, she'll wake up," I said.

"We don't know that," Mom said. "I can't feel her anymore. Maybe she isn't anywhere. Maybe she died over there and all that's left is her body and we're just keeping her from going on. I've got to think this through."

"But we know," I said. "We know where she is."

"I've got to honor her wishes."

That was it. I'd had it with her. I stormed out of the house and paced the front porch. After a few minutes, the screen door creaked open. But it wasn't Mom. Amanda. She told me I was acting like a child, which was irritating coming from a child, especially since she was at least partly right.

"You're supposed to take me to school," she said.

"Fine," I said. "Get your stuff."

"You should be nicer to Mom," she said, going back inside the house.

I paced some more. It didn't make me any less angry at Mom or myself. I walked my bike beside Amanda to her school instead of riding. I quizzed her on questions for her history test. She got them all right. I saw how she would be all through school, getting all the questions right, acing all her tests. It made me kind of proud. And then I thought how Gram wouldn't get to see any of that unless I found a way to bring her back.

"See you later, smart girl," I said when we reached her school.

"You're supposed to say 'See you later, alligator.'"

"I am?"

"Dad does when he takes me to school."

"See you later, alligator," I said.

"After a while, crocodile," she said.

A forgotten memory came back to me—Dad saying the same thing to me when I went to this school and me saying it back to him. It made me sad.

When I got to school I saw Ash out at the smoking wall, but I didn't go talk to her. I had other things to think about. Gram. Mom. Also, maybe I was a little afraid that she'd say our kissing had been a mistake. She'd thought about it. She needed a friend a lot more than a boyfriend. I just couldn't take having that conversation then.

Math. I always struggle in math, but that morning it was impossible.

History. Words, my thing. But at that moment they didn't seem to make sense. I even dozed off. I never dozed off. Mr. White had to wake me. He asked me how I could fall asleep when World War I was about to start. I didn't have an answer for him.

After class, I tried to get down the hall before Ash could catch me. I was too slow.

"I'm faster than you!" Ash shouted. "Don't make me run you down."

"Once," I said. "You beat me once."

And she'd cheated—sort of. I wasn't ready when she'd said go. She won one race and she never let me forget it.

She gave a theatrical sigh when she caught up. "Oh, God, just relax. I'm not going to kiss you again."

"You didn't kiss me the first time," I said. "I kissed you."

"Puh-lease," she said. "You don't have it in you."

"I have it and more in me."

"You don't—"

I kissed her again. That was how it happened. We kissed right out there in the hall in front of everyone and probably started a dozen rumors. It took us a while to stop, which probably started a dozen more.

"Maybe you do have it in you," she said.

"I thought maybe . . ." I said. "I wasn't sure how you would feel about things today."

"I'm feeling pretty good," she said, and took my hand. "You?"

I nodded. "About this, yeah," I said. "Not about Gram. The doctors think she's getting worse. Mom is talking about her living will."

Ash gave my hand a squeeze. "She's tough. She'll find her way back."

I knew Ash was wrong. Gram wouldn't find her way back. I would have to go get her somehow. I would have to find a way over there and make the trade. Me for Gram.

"Let's go find Emily," Ash said.

"Why?"

"Humor me," she said.

Her hand was soft against mine, and somehow that softness made me feel safe. I didn't want that to end. I knew it would soon, though.

"OK," I said.

But we didn't get the chance. Just then Detective Bloodsmith, a policeman, Emily, Eric, and another student whose name I didn't know came down the hall.

"You'd better come along, too, Jack," Detective Bloodsmith said when he saw me.

"No way am I missing this," Ash said, and she followed me following Detective Bloodsmith and the others.

We ended up in a place familiar to me, the principal's office. At least, for once, I wouldn't be the lone subject of one of Principal Thompson's uninspiring lectures.

"This ought to be good," Ash said.

Which just showed she hadn't been to the principal's office nearly enough.

35

Detective Bloodsmith took charge. He told us all to take a seat. Principal Thompson went around behind his desk. Bloodsmith stayed standing.

"I don't even know why I'm here," Eric said.

"You were having an affair with the murder victim," Detective Bloodsmith said.

"OK, yeah, we hooked up. But I didn't kill her."

"Just shut up," Emily said. "What's she doing here?" she asked, nodding at the girl whose name I didn't know.

"This is Ann Baker," Principal Thompson said. "She's a freshman here at Utopia High."

Ann raised her head from staring at the floor for a brief second.

"Do I need to call my parents?" Emily said.

"They've all been called," Principal Thompson said. "Detective Bloodsmith has assured me he isn't here to arrest anyone. He's just trying to gather information."

"Sure, he is," Emily said. "I'm not saying anything more without my parents."

"That's fine," Detective Bloodsmith said. "We can talk later down at the station. But first, tell them what you saw, Ann."

Ann kept her eyes down. She must have felt Emily's trying to burn a hole through her. "Sunday Parker got in Emily's car. That's all I saw."

"That's a lie," Emily said.

Ann said, almost too soft to hear, "No, it's not."

"Your car?" Eric said.

"Just keep quiet, Eric. Don't be stupid."

"Sure, Eric. Keep quiet," Detective Bloodsmith said. "You can come down to the station with Emily. I've probably got enough to charge you both."

"We were hooking up," he said. "That's all. It was just sex."

"Did Emily know?"

"I didn't think so then, but now I'm not so sure." He looked at her. "Am I being stupid?"

"I never cared who you hooked up with," Emily said.

I believed her. Detective Bloodsmith looked a little disappointed, so I guess he believed her, too.

I enjoyed the disappointment on Bloodsmith's face, but not enough to let Emily get away with murder.

"You didn't care about Eric," I said, "but Sunday Parker—she was different."

Emily's mouth hardened. Her cool blue eyes got cooler still.

"Go on, Jack," Detective Bloodsmith said.

"You weren't upset that Eric was sleeping with someone else. You were upset that he was sleeping with Sunday Parker. Because Sunday Parker wasn't supposed to love anyone else, was she?"

"What?" Eric said.

"Now I get it," Detective Bloodsmith said.

"But Sunday Parker liked Eric more than she liked you," I said.

Emily lunged at me, fingernails going for my face. I stepped back. Detective Bloodsmith grabbed her, and she struggled against his strong grip. Kicking. Clawing. It was like she was having a fit.

"Let go of me!" she ordered.

She kept it up for as long as she could. Then she went limp in his arms.

"That temper," I said. "That's what happened."

"I . . . I don't understand," Principal Thompson said.

"You were in love with Sunday?" Eric said, sounding disgusted.

She shrugged. "You thought I was in love with you? You're pathetic. You were useful. That's what you were."

"So what happened?" Detective Bloodsmith said.

Emily collapsed into a chair. She shrugged.

"She said she had to have Jack Bell. She wanted his heart. It was weird. Just all out of nowhere she started obsessing about Jack Bell. She didn't even know him!"

"About me?" I said.

"It was so strange how she started talking about you. She didn't even like you. Then all of a sudden she had to see you."

"Why?"

"She was talking crazy."

"Like she wasn't really her?" I said.

"Jack," Detective Bloodsmith said, "let Emily tell the story."

"She called Jack right in front of me. When he didn't pick up, she texted him and told him to meet her in the park. I know because I grabbed her phone, and when I saw what she'd sent him, I lost it. Eric was one thing, but Jack Bell? The girl wasn't even straight. I knew even if she didn't. She liked Eric, but I knew she'd grow out of him. Jack was another story. She said she had to have his heart. I just got so angry."

"You tried to make her see," Bloodsmith said.

"I told her the truth. I loved her. I told her she needed to realize who she really was; she needed to understand. You know what she did? She *laughed*! Like she thought I was joking. I lost my temper. I reached over and opened the door and pushed her out. I didn't mean to kill her. I didn't know what I was doing. I never would have hurt her."

"So how'd her body get to the park?" Bloodsmith asked.

Emily shuddered. "I stopped the car right away and went to check on her, but she was dead. I couldn't believe it. I mean, people don't die from being pushed out of cars on TV. I never thought—"

"She broke her neck," Detective Bloodsmith said.

"I freaked. I took her to the park. I don't know what I was thinking. I guess it was because she'd said she was going there."

"And," Detective Bloodsmith said, "you knew she was meeting Jack. You knew she'd called him. Maybe he'd be blamed."

"Added bonus," she said.

36

"Poor Sunday Parker," Ash said as we walked down the hall. "And poor Emily."

"Poor Emily?"

"Unrequited love's a bitch."

Tell me about it, I thought but didn't say. I did manage a little sympathy for Emily when I thought it.

"Did you get the feeling Detective Bloodsmith already knew about Emily?" she asked.

"No," I said, but then I wondered if he had and if he'd used me to out her.

"Why was Sunday Parker suddenly obsessed with you? I mean, you're not really her type."

"She's not mine, either," I said a little defensively.

"Sunday Parker wasn't Sunday Parker, was she?"

"Alice wasn't Alice. Sunday Parker wasn't Sunday Parker."

"What were they?"

"Some kind of spirit or monster. Something from the spirit world. Bloodsmith told me the handwriting changed at the end of her diary. He thought maybe someone else was writing in it. In a way he was right. Someone, something was in her."

"So you're saying both girls were, like, possessed?"

"In a way, that thing, the monster, killed them both. With a little human help."

"Why?"

"She wants me."

"Why is it every guy thinks the monster wants him?"

Before I could say anything, Detective Bloodsmith and Emily came out of the principal's office and walked past us down the hall. They were almost to the door when I shouted Detective Bloodsmith's name.

"You have that look," Ash said.

"What look?"

"All righteous. What are you going to do?"

"We have to tell him. We can't just let Brandon—I won't if you think we shouldn't, though. Your mom . . ."

"She'll be fine. The Cowboy Guru won't mess with the Russian Mafia."

"You sure?"

"Let's expose that fraud," she said.

We hurried over.

We exposed him.

"So the 'Don't do drugs' guru has his students doing drugs?" Detective Bloodsmith said.

"Definitely not good for his image," Ash said.

"So bad we think he might be willing to let Brandon go to prison or wherever to cover it up. We think he talked him into saying he pushed her."

Bloodsmith said he was going to interview some students. If what we said was true, he'd be having a talk with the Cowboy Guru soon.

37

On the way to the parking lot, I told Ash what I had figured out about both girls and then I called my mom and
told her: Both girls had died because the girl monster
wanted me. She was trying to use them somehow. Now
Gram was her prisoner. I had to stop the monster. I had to
cross over to where she was.

"Can you help me?" I said to my mother.

"I could, but I won't. I'm not losing two people I love."

"There's no other way. She won't stop. She'll kill
Gram, and she'll still come after me. Will you help?"

Silence. I was about to hang up.

"Meet me at Mrs. Morgan's," she said.

"The Wicked Witch's?" I said.

"The witch part is right," she said, and hung up.

"Where are we going?" Ash asked.

"Spirit world," I said.

"OK, then."

We got in Ash's car, and I caught her up on everything as she drove us through our sleepy little town. Though it was the middle of the day, the streets had few cars on them and the sidewalks few people. We drove by the fountain in the town's square, still going as it had been going every day of my life. I saw Mr. Goodfellow in front of the theater in a bright red traditional Chinese coat. He waved. I saw the guy who dressed as Santa Claus every year, starting long before the witches and goblins of Halloween ever had the chance to haunt our doorways for candy, because he loved Christmas so much. Our little town, quaint and full of oddly normal people who happened to have gifts—or curses, depending on your point of view.

I saw a dead man, very old, sitting on the bench in front of the barbershop, maybe waiting for a haircut that would never come.

"I would miss this town," I said to Ash.

"You think I won't?" she said, surprising me.

"I thought you were in a rush to get away from it."

"I am," she said. "But I'll still miss it."

"It's home."

"But there's a big world out there," she said, "and I want to see some of it."

"I can see it all on the Internet."

"Look, we've got about nine months before I leave. We've got plenty of time to see where our kiss will lead us. Let's just think about that for now."

"Where it will lead us?" I said warily, because what if things just kept getting better and better and then she left? Or what if they didn't lead us anywhere and then she left? Ash was my best friend, and if I lost her, I'd lose my girlfriend and my best friend all in one (fatal?) shot.

"Or we could pretend it never happened," she said, "and stay BFFs. We could do that."

The last initial and its promise of forever was tempting. What promise did the kiss have? None would be the answer. Big, fat none.

It was like in *Butch Cassidy and the Sundance Kid* (1969; writer: William Goldman; stars: Paul Newman, Robert Redford, Katharine Ross), when Butch and Sundance are trapped on a cliff and the posse of super lawmen are coming up behind them. Below them are thousands of feet of empty canyon and a rocky bottom with a narrow stream of rapids rushing through the rocks. And Butch says they'll have to jump. And Sundance says no way and then admits he can't swim. And Butch says, "Are you crazy? The fall will probably kill you."

We were on that cliff, Ash and I. The fall would probably kill us.

"What do you want to do?" I asked.

She shook her head. "I know what I want to do. The question is, what do *you* want to do? It's on you, Bell."

When we got to Mrs. Morgan's, a mansion on the bluff south of town, Ash pulled up the long drive. We rang the bell, and the cleaning lady, Mrs. Wyatt, led us into the kitchen, which in my family was where all important issues were discussed. Mrs. Morgan sat at her table, leaning on that cane that looked too much like a snake. Amanda was there, too, although Mom made her go into the living room and watch TV after we'd all said our hellos.

"All right," Mom said once she got Amanda settled in the other room. "Tell Mrs. Morgan what you told me."

I explained about Alice and Sunday and my dream about the monster. Worry lines were creasing Mom's forehead by the time I finished.

"This monster girl is too powerful, Jack," Mrs. Morgan said. "If your gram couldn't fight her, what chance would you have?"

"I have to try."

"You'll just get yourself killed. This is no ordinary spirit. Your grandmother is old, but she's a powerful witch. She's still more powerful than all of us put together. If she can't get herself out, how do you think you're going to get her out?"

"Isn't there some potion I could use?" I looked at Mrs. Morgan.

"I don't do potions," she said. "I'm a spell witch."

"OK, a spell, then?"

"My spells won't help you."

"But you can at least take us to the world of this spirit or whatever, right?"

Mrs. Morgan nodded. "And I'd call her a demon," she said, giving me a yellow-toothed smile, "but that's just me."

Demon didn't sound good. I saw by Ash's expression that she felt the same way.

"Don't scare the kids," Mom said.

A little late for that. And we weren't kids.

"Don't tell me what to do, Claire. You've been telling me what to do for twenty years. Now you want something. It's my turn to tell you. If I get your mother out of this, she and I are even. No more babysitting."

"You need me," Mom said.

Mrs. Morgan shook her head. "Your mother needed someone to watch me. So you've watched me. It's time you and I were both free."

"What's she talking about?" I asked Mom.

"Nothing."

"Demons," Mrs. Morgan said. "A little accident long ago."

I wasn't great at math, but I could put two and two together. "You were the girl, weren't you? The one Gram told me about. You summoned the demon."

She sighed. "That was a long time ago. I was a foolish teenager. Like you. I thought I could control things, but there are some things you can't control. That was a hard lesson for me to learn."

"I can handle it," I said, trying to sound confident. "Anyway, we don't have a choice."

"Mrs. Morgan's right," Mom said. "You're not strong enough, Jack. I won't lose Mom and you."

"I have to do this," I said. "She went in there because of me. And the monster is holding her because of me. It will be my fault if she dies."

"No," she said. "Not your fault. Mine. Hers. The demon's. Not yours."

"I'm doing this," I said.

I could see she wanted to tell me I couldn't. But she didn't. She turned to Mrs. Morgan instead. "All right, Diana. You go with my son and keep him safe and get my mother back and then you're free. No more babysitting. But you'll miss me."

"I'll get over it," she said.

"Library?" Mom said.

"Yes," Mrs. Morgan said.

It was a beautiful library. You had to give the old lady that. The walls were mostly mahogany bookcases crammed full of books. There was a big desk between huge French-style windows that were rounded at the top. Over a fireplace hung a picture of Mrs. Morgan's grandfather, the millionaire shipper who had built the house.

Mrs. Morgan sat in one of the golden velvet chairs over by the fireplace. She had a queen of England look to her.

"Close your eyes," she said to me. "I've been working on this passage for some time. I thought it might be needed."

"Did you see this coming, Diana?" Mom asked sharply.

"Now, where would the fun be in me telling you that?" Mrs. Morgan said.

I closed my eyes. Mom was saying we should wait. We should talk more. She didn't trust Mrs. Morgan. But it was too late for any of that. I was already in some kind of passage, a long hall. The walls were sky. It was a tunnel of sky.

"Come on, then," Mrs. Morgan said from the other end of the tunnel, where a door had appeared. "I'm not getting any younger."

38

The door opened to the north end of town, where the last houses ran into the flat shelf of white rock that went down to the Mississippi River. The rock was even whiter than I remembered. I shivered. It was cold, like I'd stepped into a freezer, like I'd stepped into winter.

Mrs. Morgan muttered something, and suddenly we both had big fur coats on. I felt better immediately. I tucked my bare hands into the coat's pockets, noticing that the world around us didn't look cold. No stiffening of the trees, hardening of the ground, ice or snow. It was like the cold came from inside us, or inside something, anyway.

Mrs. Morgan whispered to the river, and it whispered back. I couldn't understand the words, but I heard them.

A boat appeared, a cabin cruiser, and there was a man on it. A cold wind came off the river.

Mrs. Morgan said, "Come on, boy. We don't have much time."

The man wore a sailor's cap and had long black hair and a beard and a friendly, round face. He wore a blue seaman's coat with brass buttons. "Welcome to—well, let's see. What shall we call it? What would make sense to you? Let's call it . . . the Great Beyond."

"Kind of cold to be great," I said, and my words came out shivery.

The man ignored me. "I'm your captain. Hop on board and I'll take you to the queen."

"Queen?" I said. "That's what you call the mon—I mean, the woman? Queen of what?"

"Of the Great Beyond."

It was even colder than before, but still the world around us seemed the same. Then I looked at the river and saw how it was different. Not muddy brown. Clear. A mist began to rise off it and the air became milky.

"You'll take me to my grandmother?"

"I'll take you to the Great Beyond. Your grandmother is there. The queen is there, too."

I got into the boat. I held out my hand to help Mrs. Morgan in. She pulled her coat tighter around her but didn't reach out a hand and didn't move to get in the boat.

"I don't think so," she said. "You don't feel it?"

"Feel what?"

"Great, great power. There is no room for other power over there."

"We'll make room."

"There's death on the other side of the river. Your death. Perhaps my own. I've repaid my debt to Beverly. I will not go on."

The boat was already slipping away from shore. Mrs. Morgan watched us. In a second we were halfway across the river and she had disappeared in the thickening mist.

"Wait!" I heard someone call. "Come back!" It wasn't Mrs. Morgan's voice, but it was a voice I knew.

"Do you wish to go back?" the boatman said.

I didn't and I did. "Yes."

We went back to the shore. It took only a few seconds, the boat seeming to glide over the water. Ash stood right where the water met land. She was wearing a big fur coat. I didn't see Mrs. Morgan anywhere—though obviously she'd given Ash a coat.

"Go back!" I yelled, but she didn't listen. She usually didn't.

"I'm coming with you," she said.

"You can't help."

"I can help," she said.

"Just stay there. We'll be right back. You can wait on the shore."

"You need me."

"Ash—"

"We're a team. And we love each other. Unless you don't love me."

"No fair," I said.

"All is fair in—"

I asked the boatman to pull the boat to the shore. She hopped in, and immediately the current carried the boat down the river. I grabbed for the rail to steady my feet and saw schools of fish below me in the clear water. They were blue and red and green. Some were flat and wide with thick stripes. Ocean fish. The kind of fish you'd see in tropical waters.

The captain pulled out a pipe, watching us closely. Something about him reminded me of Captain Pike. Maybe just the pipe. No, it was more than that.

"Look," Ash said, tugging on my coat and turning me to look at the shore we'd just come from.

I looked back. The boat shivered and I grabbed the rail. The mist cleared behind us, and I saw that our town was gone. No modest buildings and wide sleepy streets. Utopia had been replaced by a great city of light. It was greater than any city I'd ever seen, even in films. Greater even than the Emerald City (See *The Wizard of Oz*) or Metropolis (See *Metropolis*, 1927; writer: Thea von Harbou; stars: Alfred Abel, Gustav Fröhlich, Rudolf Klein-Rogge). It had towers and palaces of gold and streets that glittered like they were made of diamonds, and everywhere the light seemed to make it glow. I could feel that the city had great and terrible secrets. I wanted to know what they were.

"What is that place?" I asked the boatman.

"It's a place that was and can never be again," he said. "Now, you be careful. The young should never want the past more than the future."

I did then, though, staring back at that lost city. I wanted everything that I would never have, things that weren't even mine and could never be mine. For a moment it all seemed possible looking at the city. Then the mist returned and it disappeared.

I knew I would dream of that city for the rest of my life.

We'd somehow made it to the other side of the river. Ash and I stepped off the boat into icy snow. It crunched beneath my shoes. Now the cold was both inside and out.

"Where do we go?" I asked the boatman.

He looked at Ash almost as if he expected her to answer. When she didn't, he said, "The palace is at the end of this road. Your grandmother is kept there. The queen will be waiting."

"Why isn't she here?" I said.

"She seldom leaves the palace."

"She can't?" I said hopefully. Limitations were a form of weakness. It made me feel a little more confident to hear she had some.

"Once no, but her power grows. The wall between the worlds has become thin."

Not good to hear.

"Let's go," Ash said. "Let's get this over with."

We'd only taken a few steps, but when I looked back, the boatman was nearly out of sight. I yelled, "How do we get back?"

"Call for the boatman!" he shouted, his voice mostly lost in the wind. "I will come."

We walked down the wide, smooth road. The world became colder still, and even the trees looked cold and brittle. We came around a turn in the road, and the road began to narrow and the forest to thicken and close in all around us. I could feel something in that forest, something watching us, and I shivered—not from the cold this time.

A second later I heard something, a growl and another growl, only they also sounded like words. The growling words were behind us and then to our side and then up ahead. A few seconds later they appeared: wolfmen. They walked on two legs. They were about seven feet tall and they had claws and fangs and fur and ears that stood high on their heads. Half man, half wolf.

We stopped, but they were all around us, snarling and snapping, speaking to one another.

"What now?" Ash said.

One of the wolfmen lunged, and I jerked back. I could feel it want my flesh.

"I'm sorry," I said to Ash.

"Tell me that you love me," Ash said.

"I love you, Ash," I said, wondering if these would be my last words. As far as last words went, they weren't bad. Then I thought of better ones. "I've always loved you."

"Now tell me that you will give me your heart," Ash said.

Something about the way she said this made me realize she wasn't speaking, you know, metaphorically (thank you, freshman English). I also realized that we weren't being eaten. The wolfmen were still talking in snarls and growls, but they weren't coming closer. Something was wrong here. I mean, more wrong than the obvious wrong of being surrounded by a pack of wolfmen.

I looked at Ash with my third eye and saw through the glamour. Her eyes were cold. Ash had warm eyes. Hot eyes. Beautiful eyes.

"Who are you?" I said.

She laughed, and it was not Ash's laugh but the laugh of a cold winter wind, of something that froze things, changed their nature. The wolfmen disappeared, and Ash became the girl I'd seen across the river in my dream, her long white hair down to her waist, her hard silver eyes, her plump mouth.

"Jack Bell. You are smarter than your ancestors. I had hoped love would make you give me your heart."

"Sorry to disappoint you," I said, not sorry at all.

"I am not disappointed," she said.

We were no longer on the road. We were in a huge room with impossibly high ceilings. The floor was smooth, glittery rock covered in places by huge thick rugs. The walls glittered, too, glowing with colors. Light danced everywhere. But it was even colder in the palace than it had been outside.

"Where's my grandmother?"

"She is waiting, somewhat impatiently, I must admit, for you to set her free. All you must do is pledge your heart to me. That is all and she may go."

"I'm guessing you're not asking for my undying love."

"More like your dying love," she said. "Well, not love. Organ. Symbolic of love. I would like you to give it willingly."

"Why do you need my heart?"

"To be free," she said. "The story is a long one and I am weary. You will forgive me if I do not go into the details."

"You killed those girls."

"My prison walls are not so strong as they once were, but I still cannot leave. I was able to use the girls' bodies for short visits to your world. Naturally I wanted a queen."

"The Corn Queen?" I said, maybe a little derisively.

"They were the most beautiful girls I could find," she said defensively. "I did not know you loved this other one until you came through the passage. Ashley. Had I known, I would have worn her. They are all so fragile, though. They burned up quickly. Their minds were not strong enough."

"I won't pledge anything until I see my grandmother."

She smiled. "You have his spirit. His . . . warmth. You please me, short-liver."

Gram appeared next to the queen. She was bent over. She looked like she was in pain.

"I wish you hadn't come, Jack," she said, breathless. "She'll send you back. You'll recover. You'll be OK."

"You shouldn't trust her."

She bent over more and grunted like she'd been punched in the stomach.

"Take care, old woman. I am losing my patience. Your heart, short-liver. Give it now and I will spare your grandmother."

"You can at least tell him why, great queen," Gram said through heavy breaths.

The queen considered this. "For Ishi. I will tell for Ishi, because this boy has much of Ishi in him. The warm eyes. The soft heart."

I looked at Gram, hoping she could somehow tell me what to do, how to fight the monster queen. But Gram stood silent, watching the queen. I could see the breath come out of her mouth like white smoke and hang in the air.

"Long ago I fell in love with a short-liver, a beautiful human. I had a mate, a king, but love is love. He caught me with the human and imprisoned us here. I could see the great city—the city of light—but I could never return, not until I had done the unthinkable: my king told me I would be free of my prison if I ate my lover's heart while he lived.

"Love made me weak. I could not eat the heart in time. You are of his line and you have his heart. I need it."

"You don't even know if it will work, do you?" I said.

The queen's eyes turned even icier, and I felt the temperature drop around me, in me. I shivered and I couldn't stop. The cold was in my bones. Guards, big men in red uniforms with brass buttons, appeared around the room.

"This has gone on too long," the queen said. "Cut her head off in the next ten seconds if the boy does not agree to give me his heart."

One of the guards grabbed Gram. The other drew his sword.

"I give you my heart," I said.

"Finally," the queen said. Then she frowned. "You must give it freely. Say 'I freely give you my heart.'"

"No, Jack," Gram said.

I have no choice, I thought.

"Yes, you do," Amanda said.

The little voice startled me. I turned and there was my baby sister.

"How did you . . . ?"

"You called me."

"Go back!" I said. "Get out of here."

"Yes, go away, little girl, or I will eat you," the queen said.

"You don't scare me," Amanda said.

I saw with my third eye that the queen was going to strike Amanda, and I just reacted. I ran at her. I tackled her. I guess I surprised her with my nonmagical attack, because she didn't react quickly enough to stop me. She hit the palace floor hard — and in that second the room began to grow warmer.

Amanda said, "Boots away."

I saw the boots on my grandfather's feet — big ones with straps and buckles I hadn't noticed before — fly off her feet.

The queen shoved me back, and I flew across the room, landing hard on the marble floor. The queen rose up into the air.

"Don't worry, Jack. Gram is a barefoot witch," Amanda said. She was next to me somehow. She helped me up without touching me. It was like the air pulled me to my feet. The girl had some skills — well, gifts. "She can fight now. Like me."

She looked down, and I followed her look and saw she wasn't wearing any shoes.

"Amanda," Gram said.

I felt them, Amanda and Gram together, making something. That something was a window. It opened. Amanda grabbed my hand and we jumped through it and Gram followed—all within a fraction of a second. Magic. Strong magic was popping and sparking light all around us.

I heard the howl of the queen as we went through the window. Amanda slammed it shut behind us.

Then we were by the river. It was cold again. Freezing cold.

"Boatman!" I shouted.

The boat came through the mist and in a second it was beside us. The boatman was smoking his pipe.

"You want passage to the other side," he said.

"Yes, please," Amanda said.

"Passage for the little witch approved, but you two," he said, looking at me and Gram. "The queen will not like it."

"Then come with us," Gram said.

"I'd have to be human," he said thoughtfully.

"Be human. Our town is protected. My granddaughter will live a long life and help protect you. Without you, the queen cannot cross."

"That's true," he said, "though it may not always be true."

"You will be warm," Gram said.

This seemed to interest him. He considered it. He considered it for longer than I would have liked. I could hear the queen in my head, feel her rage and feel it getting closer and closer.

"You and your descendants will owe me a debt, witch. I will ask for it someday."

This had a very *Godfather* feel to it (1972; writers: Mario Puzo, Francis Ford Coppola; stars: Marlon Brando, Al Pacino, James Caan).

The queen appeared behind us on the road, her wolfmen running alongside her. With a flick of her wrist, she sent them on ahead.

"Do not kill the boy!" the queen ordered. "All but the boy."

Gram turned to the boatman. "Deal," she said.

We got on just as the wolfmen reached the boat. Some jumped for it, but the boat was too swift and they landed in the water, yelping and awkwardly splashing until they went under.

The queen screamed in fury. She shouted to the boatman, "You will burn in ice for all eternity! Return now and I will forgive. Now!"

When she saw he wasn't obeying her, she began whispering to the water; only her whispers were so loud in my mind that I heard them like screams. And the water heard them, too, and began to churn and swell. Soon there was a bitter wind, and the boat was being tossed from side to side and we were being sucked back, blown back to the queen.

Gram pulled a bag from a pocket of her dress and tossed it into the water. All around us the waves rose and fell. But we were in a bubble of calm. We floated to the other side.

I helped Gram off the boat and onto land, and she leaned on me when we walked. The boatman got off after us and gave a little wave to the queen or maybe his boat, which sank the moment he stepped off it.

"You'll have to open it, dear," Gram said to Amanda as we made our way across the white rocks. "I'm too weak."

I looked around, hoping for another look at the city, but it was just Utopia, just my hometown.

Amanda waved her arms. A doorway appeared and I saw the passage of sky and we stepped in. As we did, I looked back and saw the cold queen and her wolfmen fading into the mist on the other side.

39

When I woke, I was lying on a big leather sofa. I felt Ash's hand in mine. Then she leaned over me and I smelled the musk of her perfume and her soft mouth touched mine but too briefly before she pulled back.

"How long?" I said. I hurt all over. Head, shoulders, arms. I was so tired I could hardly move. I forced myself to sit up, which caused a searing pain in my head.

"Only a few minutes," she said.

I took deep breaths and the pain in my head dulled a little.

"Just rest," she said.

"Gram?"

"Your mom is on the phone with the hospital now."

I looked over at Mrs. Morgan. She was still sitting on her thronelike chair, but she did have the decency to look a little embarrassed.

"Thanks a lot," I said.

"I got you there," she said regally.

"Where's Amanda?" I asked Ash.

"Amanda?" Ash said. "I think she's napping in front of the TV in the other room."

"But she was there."

"I don't—" She looked uncertain. Then she shouted, "Mrs. Bell! Your son's awake, but he's talking nonsense."

Mom came running into the room. She got me in one of her bear hugs and kissed me on the forehead.

"He was babbling," Ash said.

"No, I wasn't."

"Not to worry," Mom said. "He usually babbles when he's just woken up." So much for family solidarity.

"Amanda," I said. "Is she OK?"

"Of course she's OK," Mom said. "She's watching that silly movie. She just woke up from a nap."

Even though I was exhausted—encounters with monster queens who want to eat your heart are quite tiring—I couldn't help asking which movie.

"*The Princess Bride,* I think."

"That's a great one," I said. "True love. Pirates. Swordplay. Twisted, fractured fairy tale. True love."

"You're right," Ash said to Mom. "He does babble."

"You loved that movie," I said to Mom, ignoring Ash. "We watched it when I was a kid. You thought it was great."

"It was cute," she said. "You were the one who thought it was great."

"You said it was like you and Dad. Buttercup and Westley."

"Buttercup and Westley?" she said. She smiled hesitantly. "That was you, Jack. You said that we were like Buttercup and Westley."

"That sounds like something he'd say," Ash said. "He's a romantic. He doesn't like to admit it, though."

"You know, I think you're right," Mom said.

Amanda came into the room rubbing her eyes. She came up to me and jumped into my lap, hugging me.

"You're OK?" she said.

"Thanks to you," I said.

"He thinks Amanda was there," Ash said to Mom.

"I was asleep," Amanda said, and she winked at me. She was the world's worst winker, but I got the idea. She whispered in my ear, "Gram said not to tell."

Then Mom's phone rang and she answered, and I could tell it was good news by the big smile on her face.

"Your grandmother is awake," she said. "Up and demanding food, I'm told. The doctor couldn't explain it. She just came out of her coma."

When she was off the phone, Mom and Mrs. Morgan wanted to hear the whole story of my trip across the river, and I told them—but I left out one key part: Amanda.

Mom frowned. "I don't understand. You and Gram overpowered the queen?"

I remembered what Amanda had said, and I shrugged. "I had to get Gram's shoes off. I saw with my third eye that she'd be much stronger."

"That's it," Mrs. Morgan said. "Beverly's secret. She's one of the barefoot witches."

"There are more?" I said.

"A great line of powerful witches," Mrs. Morgan said begrudgingly.

"She got us out of there," I said.

Mom and Mrs. Morgan asked more questions. I answered them. I could see neither of them was entirely satisfied with my answers, but that didn't bother me too much.

Finally Mom, Amanda, Ash, and I said good-bye to Mrs. Morgan, who reminded Mom to tell Gram that she was free of her debt. I said good-bye to Ash outside, and Mom, Amanda, and I piled into Mom's car and drove down to the hospital in Dubuque. Gram was sitting up, eating. She still looked pale and tired but obviously felt good enough to complain about the food and try to convince me to go to McDonald's to get her a hamburger.

Gram asked to have a moment alone with Amanda, so Mom and I left to go get some coffee from the nurses' station. It gave me the chance to ask the question that had been on my mind, off and on, since I'd seen Bloodsmith and her that day in the coffeehouse.

"Do you love Detective Bloodsmith?"

"Don't be silly," she said. The thing was, she seemed honestly surprised by the question, which relieved me. "I may be a little confused right now, but I'm not *that* confused."

"So you and Dad aren't separating?"

"Is that what you thought?" Mom asked, reaching out to touch my cheek. (Normally I hated when she did that in public—like I was still a kid. This wasn't normally, though.) "Oh, hon, no. No, we're not separating. We love each other."

"But you were out with Detective Bloodsmith. . . ."

"Sure. He's an old friend. A good listener. Your father and I aren't separating, but we are going to counseling. We have some problems to work out. We both agree."

"That's good, I guess."

"You guess?" she said, and she squeezed my arm. "A marriage is hard work. It isn't all adventures and true love."

"I guess not."

She squeezed a little harder and squared her shoulders like she was about to take or deliver a blow. She said, "*The Princess Bride* is a movie. You do understand that real life isn't a movie."

"I understand," I said, though I sometimes wished it were.

"*The Princess Bride* is a love story, but it's a fairy-tale love story. Your dad and I are a love story, too. But a real one. Here's the thing, Jack. It's hard sometimes to love someone, hard in a way that isn't cinematic or romantic. It takes work. But it's still a love story."

"I guess," I said again.

She squeezed harder. My mom had strong hands. She had a good grip. I could have pulled away, I suppose, but I'd missed her, and, painful grip and all, I felt like she was coming back to me.

"It's still a love story," she repeated.

"OK," I said. "It's still a love story."

One of the nurses gave Mom a questioning look. I could have yelled child abuse, but I was too old for that. I smiled at the nurse.

"Tough love," I said to the nurse.

40

A few nights later, Ash and I sat on the flat white rocks by the river. The moonlight reflected off the rocks, giving them a dim white glow. The inky river, wide as ten football fields, was eerily silent.

SCREENPLAY IDEA: Zena has lived a long, long time. She kidnaps boys (for once a female serial killer) and eats their hearts. Each heart she eats gives her one more lifetime — whatever number of years the unlucky victim would have had. It's a mystery why this happens. She lives in a castle on a mountain in a remote area of Russia, but one of her cousins is getting married in New York City. She decides to go to the wedding. The cousin has never met her Russian cousin and doesn't know about her need for hearts or her age (over a thousand). But then Zena falls for her cousin's groom and she begins to question her ways. It could be a comedy/horror/action film. Maybe: *The Heartless Cousin* or *Cousin Zena Hearts New York*...

"We could go to California together," Ash said.

"Maybe."

"Hollywood," she said. "We could live in Hollywood. I could go to USC or UCLA."

"You want to go to Stanford," I said.

"It's just school. USC and UCLA are good schools."

The city of dreams. I thought of the end of *The Maltese Falcon* (1941; writers: John Huston, Dashiell Hammett; stars: Humphrey Bogart, Mary Astor), when the detective asks Sam Spade what the falcon is made of and he says it's "the stuff that dreams are made of."

"I would like to try leaving Utopia," I said, and for the first time, the very first time, I meant it.

"LA would be a better place for me to try a music career anyway," she said. "We'll both follow our dreams."

"Chase them," I said.

"Aren't you getting all brave. Leave Utopia. Chase your dream."

"I think I might be," I said.

The stuff that dreams are made of. Going to Los Angeles with Ash? If that wasn't the stuff dreams are made of, what was?

"Brave enough to kiss me without me asking you to kiss me?"

"I feel like you're asking."

She raised an eyebrow.

So I kissed her. And she kissed me back.

Acknowledgments

Thanks to my agent, Sara Crowe, for her insights into early versions of this manuscript, her confidence in my work in general, and her guidance through the perils of publishing. Thanks to all the staff at Candlewick, in particular my editor, Kaylan Adair, for her editorial brilliance and many contributions to this story, copyeditor Hannah Mahoney for her kindness and patience, and Jon Bresman for stepping in when Kaylan was on leave. As always, thanks to my wife, Frances Yansky, for putting up with me and for encouraging and inspiring me and my writing. Also, thanks to Vermont College of Fine Arts for its outstanding writing program. In particular, thanks to the following instructors: Sharon Sheehe Stark, Christopher Noel, David Jauss, Douglas Glover, and, especially, Ellen Lesser and Bret Lott. Thanks also to my writing group: April Lurie, Varian Johnson, Julie Lake, Sean Petrie, and Frances Yansky.

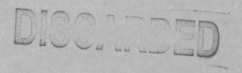